THE CITADEL

A Mystery at the Heart of Civilization

(Song of Citadels: Vol.1)

Kingsley L. Dennis

BEAUTIFUL TRAITOR BOOKS

ISBN-13: 978-1507870754

ISBN-10: 1507870752

First published: April 2015

Cover image realization - Eszter Tatay

Special thanks – Ibolya Kapta

Kingsley L Dennis, PhD, is a sociologist, researcher, and writer. He previously worked in the Sociology Department at Lancaster University, UK. Kingsley is the author of several critically acclaimed books, as well as numerous articles on social futures; technology and new media communications; global affairs; and conscious evolution. He currently lives in Andalusia, Spain.

He can be contacted at his personal website: www.kingsleydennis.com

By the same author

The Phoenix Generation: A New Era of Connection, Compassion, and Consciousness

Meeting Monroe: Conversations with a Man who Came to Earth

Breaking the Spell: An Exploration of Human Perception

New Revolutions for a Small Planet

The Struggle for Your Mind: Conscious Evolution & The Battle to Control How We Think

New Consciousness for a New World

In Your Body Is The Garden of Flowers – A Tapestry of Tales

Dawn of the Akashic Age: New Consciousness, Quantum Resonance, and the Future of the World (co-authored with Ervin Laszlo)

The New Science & Spirituality Reader (co-edited with Ervin Laszlo)

After the Car (co-authored with John Urry)

Someone asked a wise man, 'I have heard that humanity is suffering from an ailment which prevents men and women from seeing truth, from knowing themselves. What is the main symptom?' The wise man answered: 'The first symptom is to believe that one is not suffering from this illness at all. But when it really starts to take hold, the patient may agree that he is ill, but now insists that the disease is anything other than actually it is.

Idries Shah – The Perfumed Scorpion

I wish I could show you when you are lonely or in the darkness, the astonishing light of your own being.

Hafiz – The Divan

I have heard all that you have had to say to me on your problems. You ask me what to do about them. It is my view that your real problem is that you are a member of the human race. Face that one first.

Idries Shah – Reflections

Chapters

THE
SECRET
PROTECTS
ITSELF...

Chapter One - The Citadel

I grew up in the shadow of a great wall. We all did. My family was no exception. Each dawn the two suns would rise and their morning rays illuminate the sky. Yet we were all protected by the walls of the Citadel. Each day we lived in C-T was a day lived under the shadows and gaze of this imposing edifice. For many of us, like me, it became a centrepiece of our lives. Its huge structure became etched upon my mind. It was carved into the rock of my inner skull. There was no life for any of us in C-T without the Citadel.

For some the Citadel was a remnant from times past. Now it stood as an aged lifeless stone of antiquity that refused to go away. These people have all but wiped the significance of the Citadel from their minds. Each day they go about their daily routine in C-T and never stretch their heads back to peer in wonder at the towering anomaly. Their heads are kept low, as if afraid that by even catching a glimpse of the Citadel some long buried memory will be accursedly aroused. Perhaps it is fear. Perhaps it is a longing for a different present and a different past that such people live in denial.

Everybody has their own story to tell; if they tell at all. The Citadel invades all of our lives whether we accept it or not. It is as if we were all born with the design of the Citadel lodged into our very cells. No amount of forgetfulness or denial will dislodge its persistent presence within us. We all bleed red.

The Citadel walls are smooth, as if untouched. There are no signs of vandalism, and nor has there ever been sabotage to anyone's knowledge. No one has tried to breach the walls. The Citadel has been accepted without question. It's been there so long that many people no longer care to notice it. The imposing edifice remains as it always has.

No matter the rotation of our two suns - no matter how high or how low in the skies - the streets surrounding the Citadel were always provided shadow. And these four avenues, each stretching along a length of the Citadel wall, became the hub of C-T life. Within these four long avenues is where C-T life meets. These are the avenues of life, death, adventure, and experience. These are the byways where most of C-T's inhabitants live and understand their lives. These four avenues on each side of the Citadel form the playing board of our deeds. These dusty roads form the matrix where each person's life intersects, and becomes a part of others in C-T. All of us breathe these streets; the comings and goings that some of us try to discern meaning from. Some people never speak of this, or of anything related. They hardly ever make mention of those further out from C-T avenues - those who survive the onslaught of the full sun without respite. It is said that they are not real people, that the sun's heat had mutated their bodies long ago. They are sun-shrivelled outcasts that do not venture near the Citadel.

The two suns give adequate heat for us who live in C-T. Even under shadow there is strong heat. We feel it upon our skin. We have been told that if we were ever to venture out into the full light of the two suns we would be unable to see. We would perhaps eventually go blind. We have always been told this. We do not wish to blind ourselves. Those of us who live in C-T consider ourselves lucky. The Citadel gives us our canopy shade. It protects us. Life on C-T avenues moves in rhythm with the suns. When there is little shadow as the suns are overhead, then life on that avenue ceases and people stay in their homes. Activity and life circulates around the avenues like a sun-dance. The walls of the Citadel keep us close. They dominate the life of C-T. Those who speak of this protection talk in awe of the Citadel, and its founders...whoever they may have been. That was all too long ago.

But I was one of those who looked up. Who always looked up. My family and friends would joke that one day my neck would stay like that and I'd never be able to see my feet again. Yet it didn't matter. I knew that whether I looked up or not, the lights inside the great Citadel would still be shining. And that was the greatest mystery of all...the lights.

Yet what started me on my journey was the dream I had of the dying suns.

Chapter Two - The Dying Suns

It wasn't perceptible at first, just an unspoken feeling. There was a slight sense of unease between people, as if sensing a coming storm. We all came to feel, one after another, that something was amiss. Something was not right. It wasn't so much the fear of change. Despite the monotony of our world - life under a shadow - we also knew that unavoidable change could come upon us almost any time. Yet it wasn't that. It was an uncertain sense of imminent sadness. Like the slow arrival of an unwanted conclusion. It made many of us in C-T nervous; more nervous than usual. Then the shivering began.

Despite the great heat we still gained from living in the shadows of the Citadel, a few of us began to shiver. It was the first palpable sign of change. The older people noticed it first. Perhaps because of their long years of being acclimatized to C-T life they would be first to feel the

pangs of difference. In the beginning they did not speak of
this, yet they exchanged glances between themselves as if
trying to share the silent pains of a secret conspiracy. Some
of the parents spotted this growing web of silent glances
between the elders. They too did not speak of this. Perhaps
it was a form of taboo, or a way to protect us children. In
this way C-T life began to shift subtly from the inside out.
It was like an internal mutation. C-T life - our lives - was
being reprogrammed from within by some impalpable
force. We all began to change - it was inevitable. Our
moods became more sombre; there were less moments
where happiness could seep in. Days became an escape into
work, as if to avoid conversation - to avoid *the* subject.
People retreated into even more mundane distractions. The
parents, those who were the true workforce of C-T life,
spearheaded this silent takeover of our lives. Still, nothing
was spoken about this to the children. Yet we both sensed

and saw this change. Soon a conversation did arise amongst the people of C-T. It was about the changing colour.

The shadow of the Citadel had grown less dense - the elders were sure of this. At first people were dubious. They had never heard of such a thing before. It could never happen they said. The shadows of the Citadel are as consistent as the two suns, which rise and sink each day. Then the truth dawned on people with an incredible dread. The unthinkable had begun its inevitable process. The two suns were dying. Only now, after many unknown passing of sun-cycles, were the effects palpable upon the people of C-T. The shadows had protected all inhabitants from the unrelenting heat of the two suns for so long. If the suns continued to wane, as was the undeniable case, then the shadows would cease to be as strong. And they would turn from being indispensable shelter to a cloak of coldness. With the suns dying we would need their direct heat more and more. People would be forced to move out of the shadows. Yet for how long? For how many more solar revolutions would the heat sustain the people of C-T? And the Citadel - what would happen to the Citadel?

And so it eventually happened. The four great avenues that clung to the walls of the Citadel became deserted. People migrated to the outskirts of C-T where once they were afraid to go. Now they were afraid not to go. The mutants of the sun saw us coming, and left before the first wave of us arrived. We welcomed their shacks as places of refuge; as spaces of retreat. No one knew where the sun mutants had left to. Another C-T perhaps? Did one exist? The roads on the outskirts were in poor repair; neglected and dusty. They had collected the sun-drenched dust over many long cycles. Blown into corners and against makeshift walls the mini dunes had carved out in sand their own curvatures of a living shelter. It was if a different world had grown up on the outskirts of C-T; as far removed as possible from the straight-lined avenues aligned against the Citadel. Ah yes, the Citadel. Where was it now?

It could still be seen in the distance. A looming edifice: where once it stood so distinct, so permanent and imposing, it was now made blurry by the haze of the direct sun. In outline it looked like a huge ship come to moor in some dry dock; forevermore. People lamented the loss of its presence; the loss of its solid comfort. The sense of the permanence of things slowly dissolved. It was shown to us that nothing could now last forever - not even the suns. The Citadel had been so long a part of our history - built by whom? - that people could not now imagine life without it. Yet they were forced to leave their imaginations behind. The Citadel could no longer protect them; was not needed to protect them. In most peoples' eyes it had lost its function. Whatever it had been built for was now obsolete.

And yet there were some people who felt differently. It wasn't just the walls of the Citadel, they argued, it was what was going on inside that was its true function. Few listened though, not now. In the past those of the Cult of Light had a respectable following. Now their numbers dwindled to a small few as the light of the suns began to noticeably fade. Light was no more a source of inspiration and devotion. It had become a reality of lessening hope.

No one knew the source of the lights from within the Citadel. They shone from inside, day and night, without interruption or change. This was what gave people the safe feeling of permanence. High up along each side of the walls of the Citadel were rows of thin windows from where the light shone out constantly. People said they were the eyes of the Citadel. Like a living god of stone the Citadel watched over the people below through eyes of light. Yet the lights of the Citadel were never enough to pierce through the blanketing darkness of the nights. They were not meant to provide illumination for those below. This could not have been their function. Instead, they were like eyes turned inward; searching into the depths of the Citadel itself. Those of the Cult of Light said that the inner light of the Citadel sustained and nourished the inner light of humankind. As long as these lights shone, humankind would have a light inside to guide them. When they went out, humankind would lose the light of its spirit and be left adrift without a guide to home - wherever that was. Now, in the distance, it was hard to see the high window lights against the glare of two suns. In the evenings, though, under the canopy of blackness, the pinpricks of light could still be made out. This gave people some hope; but not enough.

Where once we lived extended across the great avenues as a dispersed collective, now we grew closer together amongst the shacks and dunes. First the families from the same avenues in C-T came to live closer together. Even if they had not known each other personally, they had known of each others' families. They shared what resources they had and established their own small neighbourhoods with their own laws. The rigidity of past C-T life broke down as we lived amongst the sand shelters. We began to fragment into tribal gatherings, as if retreating back into our far past. Further retreat into smaller clusters was only inevitable as the days became colder.

The weak elders were the first to suffer and die. Everybody knew the end was coming. The mood of fatalism infected each one of us like an airborne virus. We only needed to breath and the molecules of a resigned fate reached our lungs. Speaking became less and less a need between us; we saw it as a wasteful loss of energy. Only words of command and order were uttered. Words of comfort and compassion were seen as an exhausted resource. Why

counter the inevitable? Why fight a collective destiny that

came to invade? Our fate had been written upon the faces

of the two suns. In their dying they were an open book that

none could deny. C-T could not survive without the suns -

only the Citadel held that power. It became obvious that

many of us envied the Citadel. There were rumours

amongst us of attempts to gain access to the Citadel. The

Lawgivers vehemently denied this gossip and warned us

against this. And in our dying hearts we all knew such

desperate acts were futile. Never in our known history had

the Citadel been penetrated. It was not sacred - just

inviolable. It was telling that in our time of desperation our

thoughts turned to what lay inside the Citadel. When times

were good and C-T prospered there were few beside those

of the Cult of Light who ventured such thoughts. The

source of the internal light of the Citadel concerned few

people. Their external gaze fell upon other matters. Life in

C-T was fuelled by trade; it was how we interacted. It was the only way we knew how to connect – to communicate. Most items traded were useful commodities. Others traded in books, learning, luxuries; some traded only in their tales. We all had our tales. But what use were they to us now?

We all huddled closer as the coldness began to freeze the land. We could grow no more food. Our reserves of seeds were running low. The Lawgivers were forced into making difficult choices; yet priorities had to be made. The weak, infirm, and the elderly were left to meet their fate with individual dignity. The rest of us begged for rationed food with hungry eyes. We did not care for dignity, only survival. There were some amongst us who volunteered to forgo their rations for others. Why prolong the inevitable, they would murmur. It was not as if we could reverse the dying of the suns. We could expect no miracle; no rebirth. We had no gods - no idols. We worshipped those of us who were strong. We had leaders and we had those we chose to consider as leading people - both had their followers. Yet we had no collective saviour; no collective soul. All we had now was a collective sacrifice - yet to what? Those of the Cult of Light gathered in their own circle and forsook food. They were such people who had accepted the end and preferred not to struggle in vain or false hope. In their final words they spoke of the lost opportunity. As a people we had ignored the hope that had been in front of our very eyes for aeons - the Citadel. Inside there was a source of eternal light. Inside could have laid the answers to our greatest questions - not only to our survival but to our meaning. And we had forfeited this hope. As if living in the kingdom of the blind we had traded our lives upon C-T avenues, oblivious to the true nature of the edifice that gave us shelter. The dying of the suns, they said, was a gesture in our final humiliation. Then they fell silent; and were lost to the encroaching ice.

Dusty streets were a faded memory. The cold made it harder for our minds to remember, and for our mouths to speak. Fewer families huddled together in ever smaller spaces. The avenue tribes had finally melded into the tribe of humanity. Fires were lit yet only served to appease a slither of surface chill. Deep down our bones were freezing. It was an internal chill we could not escape from. Soon not even the fires could help us feel anything. We had become numb to life. Life ebbed away as the ice encased us. We were no more. Our C-T wiped from all conscious memory. Our world - a frozen remnant of life that failed to succeed.

Only the Citadel remained.

Chapter Three - The Calligrapher

The dream stayed etched upon my mind. It was almost real to me. I had woken up shivering. Not from the anxiety of the dream but from the cold. I had felt it squeeze into my bones. I felt the cold void as the ice entombed us, and we could speak no more. I had watched as our collective soul was extinguished as if a fragile candle flame. Upon waking I could not be sure which world was truer. I stumbled to the window to peer outside, and sighed in relief at the sight of the Citadel rising before me. The dawn shadows falling from the great walls embraced me, as if to say that everything was well - for now. I knew then that the Citadel had called me; it had reached out to me. I could not believe that something so close, so monumental - so intrinsic to our lives - could be so utterly unknown.

I am young in years, and am soon to finish my cycle of
study. Many of us young ones begin an apprenticeship
shortly after studies finish. If I could, and if I had a choice,
I would wish to be apprenticed to the Calligrapher.
Calligraphy appeals to something within me; and the
Calligrapher is a man of respect, as well as something of an
enigma. Before the two suns rise and fall another twenty
times I shall have finished my studies and be considered
ready for my next stage. For now many of my days are
allowed to me in free time. Each day is filled with the
interplay of sun and shadows; they move together in
orchestrated rhythm. The shifting of sun and shadow
defines each day for us - our time of work, rest, and sleep.
We are a people - a C-T - tied to the shifting celestial
spheres. We often forget that we do not exist alone, such is
our arrogance at times. We only need to remind ourselves
of sun and shadow to know that we are indelibly bound to
a greater movement. Our lives in C-T, by comparison, are

but the tiny markings upon a dusty track within some miniscule moment.

My sun days, when I am not in study, are spent a great deal in wanderings, meetings, and errands around C-T. I often help my father by delivering by hand his documents to the necessary people. My father is a Keeper of Records, and works with the group of C-T Archivists to preserve accurately most of the things that happen in and around C-T. I once asked him if he knew the history of the Citadel - who had built it and when, and for what purpose. He looked at me with glazed eyes and shook his head. It was as if the question was outside of the archives; outside of any known archives. Perhaps it was a question for which no answer exists. Or maybe we have just been asking the wrong questions all this time. I've always had questions; more questions than there were answers for. Once I had wanted to become a Keeper of Records like my father. Then I was told that this would never be possible for me. Besides, I was informed that families cannot pass on the same trade - it leads to a specialization in families. The C-T needs diversity; we must try, they say, to avoid a centralization of power. I'm not really sure what that means. What use is power when we are all huddled beneath the walls of the Citadel? Surely anything such as power must reside in the knowledge of the Citadel and who we are as a people? Control over ignorance is not really power, as I see it.

I called in on the Calligrapher, as I often did. His small dwelling served as both his home and his workshop. This was normal. In the lack of space in the avenues around the Citadel there was often only room for one abode for each family and their trade. Only the males operated a trade. The women worked at everything else. To me it always seemed

as if the women were busier; their life and their work never

seemed to stop. If I could name their trade I would call it

'Life.' I often wondered why C-T thought so highly of their

trade and so little of their 'Life.' Perhaps this is one of the

consequences of living in a place, a society, where the men

seem to have the power. I don't see it that way. Yet that's

the way that C-T explains it. And it's the way people speak.

Again, it's not something I fully understand or which

interests me. I hear people speak a lot, about many things

in C-T life; yet they each speak the same. You listen to one

and you've heard the C-T conversation. There is not much

variation. I sometimes think that C-T controls people's

conversations, or rather their thoughts. Perhaps everything

is a grand illusion and we are all living in some giant

invisible dome where no outside thoughts can penetrate in.

We live each day with the same thoughts passed from

generation to generation; with only a few extra bits added

each time for a bit of newness. The story of our past has
not changed much. It's like an endless procession of sun
days interspersed with our constant shadows. Yet it is the
shadows that protect us. When I look up into the night sky
I see the sprinkled dots of a thousand suns like ours - and I
want to reach out to them. There is nothing worse than
having a mind that dares not leave behind its terrestrial
world.

I entered quietly into the Calligrapher's shop so not to
disturb him at work. The old man often worked in a back
room in solitude. In the front room of the Calligrapher's
dwelling stood a young boy who was his new apprentice.
His function was to greet those who entered and to pass on
messages to the old man. Knowing me from my several
visits he waved me into the back with a friendly smile. The
Calligrapher's working room was cluttered with his

materials - brushes, paints, canvases. There was order in the Calligrapher's mind, this I knew from speaking with him. Yet his external surroundings showed the disorder that, he once told me, reflected the disorder of our human-made reality. The essence, he said, was still and pure, and could not be ruffled - not even by the chaos of the charade of human minds. I remember him saying that we etch our wishes, dreams, and sufferings, upon the canvas of the cosmos. And with each cosmic wind the canvas is wiped clean. Only the remnants remain in the human collective soul, like some grand archive. He turned to me now and nodded. My presence was acknowledged and accepted. I did not need to be here, yet I came nonetheless. I had a sense that I could learn more by being in this man's presence than by scuttling along the shadows of the Citadel walls. Other young peoples' voices become muffled against the bricks of the great walls that tower over us. My voice I keep silent, so it speaks to me with a clearer voice within.

Life in C-T is distracting; it plays upon us everyday. For what reason I do not know. I know little about reasons. I feel there is something beyond our reasons, for which we have to reach out for if we ever wish to know. Without asking - without reaching - there will be nothing more here than life in C-T. And the shadows of the Citadel.

'Your eagerness is impressive.' The Calligrapher looked up from his drawing and peered over at where I sat. I nodded back. I felt he understood me, and was pleased at my presence. There was a silence between us that was both necessary and appropriate. Creating the lines upon the canvas, he had once said, was a silent communication between the inner heart of the Calligrapher and the subject. Without this, the subject can neither be truly known nor represented. Everything else, he said, was space.

'You come here, not only to learn, but because nothing else feeds you.' The Calligrapher's eyes were young despite his years. His age, whatever it be, was kept tucked away behind his orderly grey beard and wrapped under his darkened skin. Like me, he too it seemed, had many questions of his own. Or maybe all the long hours in quietude brightened the depths of our unknowing and released our longing. In C-T life there existed much longing of a different kind; and much quenching of this false longing.

'You must learn to feed others if you are to find success in this art. People think they come here because they appreciate beauty. Yet they do not know what beauty is. They are attracted by form; by the shadows of beauty. Just as we live under the shadows of some greater truth. And for such people the shadows of beauty are enough to quench their tepid desires. Like their desires, they too are impermanent. Yet it is the duty of the Calligrapher to give what he can. We are providers, givers - it is our service. A Calligrapher is always in service. We must remember our responsibility to others. We provide what they ask of us; and more. It is for us to interpret what people really ask for when they come here with their requests. These requests are not yet fully-formed. They are outlines; glimmers of some deeper urge they can neither recognize nor name. Their deeper longing can only manifest in unformed wishes for a pretty symbol, or an arrangement of words. For them it is an emblem of a life - something to hang in their dwellings to bring them comfort where there is nothing else. For the Calligrapher, it is different. We know that each creation from our brush is a trigger for a person's soul to breathe. We provide this contact. This connection is slight; yet it is better than complete forgetfulness. Why people should need such subtle signs when we live in the light of the Citadel is beyond me.' The Calligrapher noticed that my eyes had widened and I had begun to lean in closer. He smiled, and allowed a small yet audible chuckle to seep out.

'Yes, the Citadel interests you. I know it does.' The Calligrapher's soft voice filled the room even though he spoke quietly. He went back to his work; drawing with precision his careful lines as if they carried some heart in their tincture. It amazed me each time to observe his careful and focused concentration, as if each moment was both temporary and yet eternal. The Calligrapher seemed to know how to stretch time as if it were some tangible substance he could incorporate into his design. After several minutes of uninterrupted silence the Calligrapher paused and took his brush away from the canvas.

'Most people here live by the shadows; their lives are dominated and ruled by shadow and shade. They are either afraid or do not know how to live in the light. It is the conditioning of C-T. This keeps us bound by the forces of denial, and not by affirmation. To be a true Calligrapher you must live by the light. We live under the light of the Citadel - not its shadows.' I nodded. I wanted to affirm each word the Calligrapher was speaking. I felt each word to have its own rightness. Just as each line from the Calligrapher's hand has its rightness and precision.

'You have many questions,' said the Calligrapher as he nodded thoughtfully. 'It is important that you do not replace these questions with answers. Answers close the mind. They produce an energy of closure and we fail to seek for more; they bring death to our questions. A true question has no death - it is eternal.' The Calligrapher went back to his intricate design, peering close to the canvas as if his eyes desired for a tangible touch. I stood up and walked over to where he was seated. From behind his hunched figure I could see a richly drawn design where coloured strokes coalesced into a startling symbolism. I was awed, and knew I had much to learn from this old man.

'Learning is about seeing,' spoke the Calligrapher, as if sensing my thoughts. 'Everything has something to tell us. There are clues woven through all the ineffable intricacies of our lives. Let me illustrate this with a story: There was once a tinsmith who was unjustly accused of a wrongdoing and falsely imprisoned. Now this tinsmith asked the prison guards if they may allow his wife to bring him a rug so that he could meditate daily, as was his custom. The guards agreed, since they liked this gentle and agreeable man. Soon a rug was delivered and the tinsmith would meditate daily in peace and calm. After a short while the tinsmith again approached his guards with another request. "I am a poor tinsmith," he said, "and yet I have a humble skill which could be put to use for our mutual benefit. I am a man of my work, and to create gives me meaning. Whilst I am here

in this cell I am losing my sense of meaning. If you could
bring me some tin and a few tools I could make small
objects which you could sell in the local markets. You
could keep the profits for yourself, and I would have
something to do to occupy my days." The guards discussed
this among themselves and agreed to this harmless offer. In
the days that followed the guards were able to receive the
small decorative objects and make some extra money for
themselves. They were pleased with this new venture. Then
one day when they came to inspect the tinsmith's cell they
found the door open and the cell empty. They could not
believe how this could be possible. They were completely
mystified. Years later when the tinsmith's innocence had
been recognized and a public apology issued, one of the
guards ran into the tinsmith. "How did you ever escape
from your cell?" he asked. "It is a question of design and
meaning," answered the tinsmith - and then he explained
what he meant. "My wife is a weaver, and she must have

spoken with the locksmith responsible for the prison locks.
As I was in meditation daily upon the rug I began to notice
that an intricate design was woven into the rug - the design
that resembled that of a lock. And I am a tinsmith. It was
in my capacity to create with my tools, which you allowed
me to have, a key for the lock. It was a matter of design,
awareness, and capacity. It all fitted together - like a lock
and key!"

The Calligrapher smiled at his own story as he returned to
his brush strokes. I could see more clearly now how the
outer surface of the canvas concealed a more intricate
design. There were lines that seemed to conspire against
the eyes. Such lines were asking for another sense to
approach, and reach out. Only in this more subtle manner
would the lines reveal their secrets. The Calligrapher looked
up at me and met my gaze.

'The secret protects itself,' he said softly. At that moment his young apprentice entered the studio and informed us that a client wished for an audience. The Calligrapher nodded for the client to be brought in. I went to stand over to one side of the room. Shortly a large man with broad shoulders stooped through the low doorway and expanded himself into the room. He briefly glanced at me yet afforded me no recognition. I was still young and without status in his eyes.

'I want you to draw me a phasal bird. They are rare creatures, as you know. I am sure you can find out what they look like if you search in the archives.' The man spoke roughly, with little courtesy or graceful manners. The Calligrapher closed his eyes for several moments and then nodded.

'I am aware of the phasal bird. It is a beautiful bird that no longer graces our sun-filled skies. I can draw one for you.'

'How long will this take you? And what is your payment?'
As ever, the Calligrapher showed calculable and measured
calm.

'Your drawing will be ready when thirty dawns of our two
suns have passed. Your payment shall be according to your
pleasure and appreciation.'

'This is a long time for one drawing. I thought it would be
less.' When the Calligrapher did not reply the large man
nodded curtly and left the room. The Calligrapher leaned
back in his chair and met my eyes with a steady look.

'Time is something we do not yet know how to measure. It
eludes us, and yet we cling to its power. We are unaware of
how time truly functions. And people are worried that time
dictates their value of payment. Life in C-T is based on
trade, yet it has sadly lost the knowledge of exchange.' The
Calligrapher slowly rose from his chair and beckoned me to
follow him. His bent frame passed easily through the low
doorway as we entered the front of the dwelling. He looked

behind at me and a nurtured smile spread across the thin line of his lips. We both stepped outside and under the shadow of the great wall.

'Here, beside the great living heart of C-T, people trade in dead value. Humanity no longer values true exchange. Now we place a different value on what we can get; and that value is a shallow thing within the intangibility of time. If we do not change our ways then C-T will decay. Its structures will crumble into the dust at our feet. Our humanity, our great experiment, will fade into myth. And then it will fade into the void. The two suns will search again; and other sons of the sun will come forth. Throughout all of this the Citadel will be waiting. Its internal lights will never grow dim. The source will be still and patient, knowing that there will come those who seek to enter. Any civilization that lives upon the ephemeral must dissolve in the long run. It has no place amongst the suns of our eternal home.' The Calligrapher turned to

hobble away. 'But *you* still have time. You are not needed

here yet.'

I watched him shuffle back inside. I felt a slight tightness

in my chest. I looked up at the towering walls of the

Citadel. Far above I could just make out the slits that were

the high windows - where the internal light shone

constantly. I breathed in deep and moved on.

Chapter Four – The Smithy

The Smithy had his workshop along the same avenue as the Calligrapher. Yet their work could not have been any further apart. Whilst the Calligrapher delicately passed his brush across the canvas, the Smithy banged his metal into being. The fire of his forge burned constantly - ever ready for work. The Smithy and his two apprentices sweated out each day by the fire and heat of transmuting metals. Theirs was a hard and dirty work. Much needed and yet little appreciated. The Smithy, a tall, lean man with strong arms, carried with him a solemn face. To smile would be to admit that life contained secret joys. For him it did not. C-T appeared to be a thing to challenge; an opponent of greater force that kept the Smithy at bay. His hammering seemed to reflect his own personal struggles with a world he did not, could not, understand. Conformity came as a relief; a space of retreat and compromised shelter. Yet underneath everything I sensed a ripple of fear, and a deep, etched reticence. On this day I was to be proved more than right. Not that I wanted to.

'Ah, the child of Johan.' The Smithy acknowledged me in a flat, thin voice that was neither a welcome nor a question. It was like he had spoken a fact; just as dryly as if he was reading from the archives. My presence amongst the workers here was no surprise. I had wandered between them on several occasions previously. They recognized me for my curiosity. I even think that silently they welcomed me there. I was an added presence; some new element amongst their monotonous work. I did not interfere with their work or disturb them. I knew how to keep out of their way whilst still maintaining my presence. This, I sensed, they initially tolerated; then gradually they came to welcome it. People in C-T can move about freely to visit and speak with others - whether for study or for personal relations. It is a matter of individual choice between each of us whether we welcome a person or avoid their company. My father Johan is well-respected as a Keeper of Records, and his work with C-T archivists is highly regarded. As a result, my movements have been more free than many; and my presence more welcomed, or tolerated.

'Child of Johan. The one who is still curious – you return yet again.' The Smithy was speaking both to me and about me in his detached manner that I have grown accustomed to. The Smithy's tone is neither disparaging nor friendly. It is an odd tone of neutrality that seems to match his dispassionate air. How can such a man, I wonder, create such important tools, and with such skill and craft? The Smithy's work is highly praised throughout C-T. They say his work surpasses that of the previous Smithy. The Smithy's work is lauded for its attention and sense of rightness. And yet in the man himself, in his personality and energy, I find little of distinction. The man must only live through his metalwork, his products; and so meagrely through a human life. Despite this, there is something in the Smithy that attracts me. Perhaps it is his state of neutrality that spares him further pain and makes him amenable to me. He has not the care to criticize, nor the want to engage in idle chat. The Smithy is innocent of gossip, and seemingly devoid of malice. Yet within himself there is fear: a fear of living that shrinks this man to a shadow. Maybe it is fitting that he finds solace in the shadows of the great wall. For him, life is a perpetual shadow; and hopes a thing beyond human reach. The Smithy is resigned to a fate of crushing normalcy. Yet within this clamp he is able to produce the finest metalwork of incredible precision. It is this capacity of production under such stressful personal antagonisms that endears the Smithy to me. Still, I cannot ignore the energy of fear that clings to him.

'Child of Jchan. Come. See and listen here. There is more for you.' I followed the Smithy as he walked from his workbench toward the back of his workshop. There is heat around us that engulfs us in equal density. The Smithy moved toward a workbench and motioned to it casually with his hand. I observed the objects spread across the workbench; they were strange and unusual to me. I am not a trained eye in metalwork, yet I sensed unfamiliarity in these symbols. They appeared to be instruments of some kind. Perhaps they are to measure something, or to map some unknown distances. Their symbolic construction spoke of uncommon knowledge. I looked away and into the rigid face of the Smithy. His steady gaze noticed my interest and curiosity.

'I thought these would interest you.' The Smithy kept his focused gaze upon me. I thought I saw a slight upturn at one corner of his mouth. A self-satisfactory smile perhaps? I nodded in agreement to him. He is right, of course. I *am* interested. I do wish to know more. I continued to stand there looking at the array of unusual yet finely crafted instruments. I was unsure whether the Smithy would allow me to touch them. I did not wish to interfere with another person's work.

'I was given the designs to make these - a special order. They are for the Cult of Light. They are connected with the Citadel. I know you are interested in the Citadel - more than most of us are. More than is healthy too, I say.' I looked back at the Smithy and his gaze was still upon me, as if measuring me for a precise metallic instrument. Perhaps these instruments here were the personal profiles of people, rendered into metallic objects for eternal archiving. Maybe the Smithy wanted to allure me here as a trap, to kill my young body and sculpture it into metal? I brushed these idle thoughts away. They were but the shavings of an overactive mind. I knew the Smithy was reaching out to me, wanting to tell me something. Yet he finds it difficult to communicate in words. It is not his language. His tongue has no place in a furnace where the heat and human muscle bangs physical objects into shape. Words cannot shape the objects that the Smithy works with. And so this organ has petrified through lack of use. I sense there is something locked away in the Smithy that cannot be released. Perhaps through his banging and shaping he finds some escape. I returned his concentrated gaze. I wished to acknowledge him; to let him know I understood his efforts.

'The Cult of Light feels our civilization is dying; that we are no longer a living civilization. They say it is because we have lived in the shadows too long. Inside we have become like shadows they say. Our only hope lies in the Citadel - in the source of its light. This could be our light.' The Smithy looked away. I did not know whether it was through shame or embarrassment at these words that he turned his head. At that moment loud banging from the workers reached our ears. Our thoughts were smothered in the clashing of metal against softer metal. Is our civilization dying I wonder? Do these instruments, these metallic objects, make a difference? Can we bang and force our way into the future? The Smithy beckoned me to follow him as he moved into a small side room away from the noise. He took a battered flask from a small metal table and poured some liquid into a metallic mug, which he then offered to me. He poured another for himself and sat down at the table. After a few seconds I joined him on the chair opposite and brought the warm liquid up to my mouth. It had a sweet taste to it…a stream of sweetness within a place of grime and sweat. The contradiction made me smile inside. Even if our civilization is dying, I thought to myself, there are still places of sweetness within each of us, despite the dirt.

'I have never understood the Citadel. I didn't try to. It was not something that was important in our family. We thought it idle talk…for minds with too much time. It was nothing more than a building. We believed in C-T. In the laws and ways of trade. What we did not understand, we did not understand. There was no yearning after ghosts.' The Smithy's face looked weary and drawn as he supped from his mug. I could sense there was more within him, yet locked back as if by some invisible belt around his chest. He was struggling for the words; wrestling within to find expression for the intangible. All his life he had worked to forge the tangible. Now he was at a loss when faced with the ephemeral, the untouchable. A part of me wanted to reach out and touch his hand. Just a slight touch; to let him know it's okay. But I knew this was not possible between us. Not in this environment where strong physical force reigned. Perhaps it was in this tangible world where the decay had first begun.

'One of them came here...from the Cult of Light. They had plans, drawings, for the instruments. Very precise. Easy to follow; but not easy to understand the work. I think I have done a good job. It is the best I can do. I work with my hands, not my mind.' I felt a tinge of resentment coming from the Smithy at the obligation he had been put under by the designers of these instruments. It was a feeling of unfairness that I sensed. Maybe also a fear of failure at not being able to deliver? A Smithy in C-T should always be able to deliver. I sensed it was a hard task for this man.

'They want to find a way into the Citadel. They want to scale its walls, to scrape at its structure!' The Smithy's mouth tightened as he said these words. His eyes narrowed too - a mixture of disgust and frustration. He sighed. 'They want to reach those windows. It's the light. They are desperate about the light. They think that if the lights go out, we will all perish. But...but no one goes into the Citadel. There is only the same, the same.' The Smithy lowered his head until his gaze met the floor. There was a silent moment of joining and separation, or separation and joining.

'There is only the same, the same...,' muttered the Smithy under a low breath. I did not know what he meant. I could not know. Yet I saw a flash of fear return to his eyes. I gently urged him to tell me more.

'It is a Smithy's tale. We all know of it. It is passed down in our Guild, but discreetly. We sometimes used to speak of it quietly amongst ourselves. But fewer times it has been spoken recently. There are few ears who would be keen. I am less keen too. Yet I know of your interest, child of Johan. This may be a tale for you. In telling it I may find some unknown purpose.' The Smithy paused and fell into a natural silence. He was reaching within his depths to retrieve the parts of his story; to refit and animate them together into a coherent whole he could transmit. Transmitting through words was a difficult thing for him. I appreciated his effort. A delicate ripple traversed his thin lips, almost imperceptibly against his thin, taut face.

'In our Guild many two-sun cycles ago there was a man unusual for a Smithy. This Smithy would tell wondrous stories to everyone who listened. He was even known to sing, whistle, or hum his stories. He was a cheerful and happy man, somehow unsuited to the life of a Smithy. Yet he was also good at his trade. In those days there was more social mixing. People of the various trades and guilds would come together and share stories. They say that in those times the Citadel was respected. They say that people spoke of its power to sustain us. Yet this Smithy spoke of more than one Citadel. He told and retold a story that he said had been handed down in his family for generations. It was known as the "Song of Citadels" - and it told of other places, beyond our horizon, where other Citadels stood in protection of its peoples. It was a story that sang of hope, of brotherhood; of humanity amongst the stars. It was a great story that, they say, people asked the Smithy to repeat many times.' The Smithy could see that I had a quizzical look on my face. He seemed to know exactly what I was thinking.

'Why is the "Song of Citadels" not known today? Why has no one heard of it outside of the Guild of Smithies? The reason is that the Guild has forbid it. It has disappeared from public circulation. And now all but disappeared from the minds of men and women. The Guild considered it dangerous. The tale is no longer spoken in our Guild, yet we sometimes quietly whisper amongst us of what happened. Only by our mouths will this story survive. No records exist in our archives or any archives. Even the Lawgivers of C-T do not possess the "Song of Citadels." Why now? You are perhaps wondering why I tell this story now? The truth is, I feel something similar is coming to pass. Here, soon, with us in C-T. This story could have warned us…could have helped us prepare. But no. The Guild thought it knew best in wiping the existence of this story from memory. Yet once something has existed, it leaves behind traces. Somewhere. Like us, here and now.'

The Smithy poured two more mugs of the hot sweet liquid and leaned forward with his elbows upon his knees. He drew in his breath.

'A long time ago, yet not far from where we are seated now, a Smithy knew the "Song of Citadels." He would recite it often, to the many who came and asked. He told a story of a place over the horizon, where the suns do not show us. A place where there is another Citadel, and life is happy. It is a mirror of our future, where humankind has harnessed its full powers and where progress is advanced. It is a place where people want and lack for nothing. It is a place that came before C-T, and was its ancestor long ago. The Citadels are said to be the custodians of humanity. This Smithy talked so much about this place - the name of which I am forbidden under oath to reveal today, or any days. One day, as the Smithy was re-telling his story it was said that a man from a rival Guild challenged the Smithy's account. This challenger called the story a fantasy, and our Smithy as a fraud. He called out the integrity of a fellow guild member. Our Smithy had to respond, or forego his reputation. The Smithy announced that every word was true, upon the honour of his family and forefathers. For this was their family story, and known amongst them for generations. The challenger did not relent. Again, he denounced the Smithy as giving false account and as a man of weak constitution. If the story was true, said the challenger, then the Smithy must prove this or forfeit his honour. The Smithy must travel to this place, to this other Citadel, and prove its existence. By now the audience were caught up in the mass emotions of the challenge. They were eager to know of this other Citadel. Maybe they were greedy to know of the future. Men are such as this.' The Smithy looked over at me to see if he still had my attention. I nodded to reassure him he did. A brief silence emerged between us that was as natural as a two sun dawn. The heat from the workshop was still enclosing us. I could feel the few bubbles of sweat on my forehead as a reminder of where I was. Yet we as people were accustomed to heat. It was the cold that we feared. My concentration was fixed upon the Smithy's thoughtful figure. He was still sat slightly bent over.

'The Smithy arranged for his departure, with food and protection against the suns. Those of the Guild saw him leave. They did not approve of this adventure, yet they could not allow a challenge against them go unmet. It was said the Guild elders were deeply concerned. Yet it was done. And the Smithy was gone. He must have walked beyond the perimeters of C-T, and out beyond where the few sun mutants dwell. Out beyond the threshold of all known dwellings. It was a brave adventure. The Smithy was a brave man.' The Smithy sighed as if remembering a brother. 'Nothing was heard of him for a long time. For a very long time. Some spoke of his demise. Those of the Guild were close to forgetting the adventure when a ragged figure appeared on the outskirts of C-T. The Smithy had returned. Somehow he had made it back. But he did not return as the same man. He was different, changed. He looked older…much older than his years. And there was, they say, a deep trouble nestling inside of him that had half-eaten him away. He was a partial man. He could smithy no more. He returned to his dwelling and locked himself away. He did not want to see anyone. When he did not present himself before the elders of the Guild of Smithies, they came to him. This Smithy told the guild elders that after many trials and difficult trekking, he at last passed our horizon and onto another plane. In the far distance of this land he indeed saw a Citadel, out there where the lazy eye escapes to. He saw too the shapes of another C-T beneath its walls. With great effort yet eager heart he walked into this place, hoping to be greeted well. He was indeed greeted, yet what he saw shocked him.' The Smithy again paused. His eyes seemed to swim as if they too were lost upon some far horizon.

'Everyone, he said, was the same as us here in this C-T. For every one of us here, there is another one over there. We are multiple, we are not only ourselves. Yet what was worse, the Smithy said that this other C-T was in great decline. People had stopped believing. They had no hope, no trust in the future. They cared only for the last remaining possessions to bring them power. And when the Smithy looked up at the high walls of the Citadel he saw that the windows shone no light. The light of the Citadel had gone out. And he returned home to this C-T a broken man. The Guild did not believe his story - they could not. They decided the sun had made him mad, had altered his senses. He was delusional they announced. They left him alone to his fate. He lost his family for he cared for nothing. He grew old fast. He died quickly. And his story was not told publically by the Guild. It has remained within our walls as our secret. Now too this is dying. There are fewer Smithies now who know fully of the "Song of

Citadels." This too will pass.'

The Smithy stood up and made to leave the room. He

glanced behind at me to see if I would follow. We re-

entered the workshop and immediately the heat of the

furnace leapt upon us. I felt a new sweat emerge, and with

it a new taste. The Smithy was more accustomed to this

environment than I. There was hardly any sweat upon his

brow. It was as if his lean face was proofed against

perspiration. We walked up some metal spiral stairs that

delivered us to the rooftop. The two suns were still low in

the sky at the other side of the Citadel. Our avenue was

comfortably in shade. We remained protected. In that

instance I felt something I had never felt, or imagined,

before. I saw the Citadel as a mother. A great stone mother

than protected and nurtured her children. And we, her

children, were ignorant of this great sacrifice - ignorant of

this Great Mother. And our C-T, our ways, they were

etched in manhood and masculine law. I felt a deep drop in

my stomach. I felt a bodily certainty of truth that

manifested in an internal constriction. My muscles had

reacted to a thought, an inspiration. Never before had I felt

this. Never before had I had this thought. Now my whole

body tingled as if an electrified knowing had caught me in

an ethereal embrace.

The Smithy stood by the low stone wall at the roof's edge.

His thought, like his gaze, was surely cast outwards. Across

from us both rose up the magnificent edifice. She (now I

say she) was truly beyond remarkable. I reached out my

hand and gently touched the Smithy upon his arm. It was a

brief gesture, a connection. It was something that existed

only then, for that such briefest of moments. Then I pulled

back. I knew the Smithy would not have tolerated a longer touch; even if he had wanted to. It was not in our ways. It was not my way - until that moment. I sensed something had touched us both. As if an emanation of some energy were reaching us from the Citadel. Urging us; for something...something else, or other.

'I know now why they had to hide that story. Why we could talk no more of that other place - the other Citadel.' The Smithy did not turn to look at me as he spoke. He remained gazing out away from the roof. 'If that was our future, then what hope is there? If it was a warning, then it has passed unheeded. The demand for my metals increases. I see the demand for stories has disappeared. Little of the past is spoken about within families or guilds today. We have no human story. We are not together - we are alone.' As he said these final words the Smithy turned and shot me a brief glance. He walked past me, pausing almost imperceptibly as he did so. There was a split moment when something had come to him. Yet he had dismissed it.

I was left alone on the roof, with the Smithy's words in my body.

Chapter Five - The Archivist

I stayed a moment longer on the rooftop to allow the Smithy's parting words to sink within me: *we have no human story*. Did it finish, or did we lose it? I could give no response. The Citadel looming across from me now seemed to hum and vibrate as a written narrative in stone. There was our history – our story – etched into her mineral body. Yet we could not see it. We did not have the sight. How can one touch a seemingly intangible thing? But there she was – a glorious structure. Haunting us whilst we were taunting ourselves.

The Smithy's workshop was behind me, left to its noise and intrusive smells. The day was still in its first half, with the two suns rising slowly upon the other side. I had seen it many times, how the bright sunlight slowly crept up one wall only to descend upon the other. If we could put markings upon the Citadel walls we would be able to measure each moment of the day. The Citadel would serve us as some huge timepiece that regulated our passing time. Yet this too would be converted by human minds into another tool to manage and control our C-T lives. As it stands, we know our movements, our contacts, our activities by the progress of the two suns upon our canvas overhead. I have wondered if we are within some dome, and our two suns are artificial orbs created to regulate our days. Just as the Citadel is an artificial monolith placed here for some as yet unfathomed reason. A test? Or a map perhaps? There could be other beings inside observing us, monitoring us. Are we entertainment for them – or maybe some kind of experiment? Perhaps they are looking out at us, knowing we never have the instinct to try to peer within. We scuttle across the sandy floor of silent streets. We are giving the human story to them; and at the same time it disappears away from us. Out of our hands into theirs.

The two suns were reaching near their mid-point zenith as I stood outside the Archivist's dwelling. The Archivist is a friend of my father. They have shared many stories together; sometimes by speaking, other times by archives. I have listened to some of their conversations. I am sure this was where my own questioning was birthed. Amongst the words passed like medallions between minds that searched and shared. In the intangible unknowing I caught a whiff of the soul smell. My nose has always been stronger than the power of my voice. The archivists are not supposed to question the information that passes between them. They are the carriers and the collectors – they cannot interpret. Such positions – such minds even! – are functional. My father Johan remembers much yet speaks his own mind very little. I imagine it is like having a ball of mud in your hands and not being able to mould it into other shapes. It remains always a ball of mud, and nothing else will come from it.

The Archivist looked up from his desk as I entered and chuckled. His large cheeks extend his rounded face as I have seen it often; bent in archives. And now his balding head shimmered in sweat; the physical baubles of his own work. The mind is an engine that produces its own heat. Some of this heat is stored as information. Other heat is interpreted as thoughts. My thoughts too are a product of this internal mental heat. In comparison the rest of our bodies are cold. Here I feel is where our emotions lie; stretched throughout us as an extended mind. Emotions are the instinctive body, communicating under our skin through chemicals and molecules. They are harder to find;

and even harder to fathom. Instead, the heat from our

minds becomes the main tool of our communication. And

for us it becomes the core of our civilization. The men of

C-T have extended the rule of the human mind through

countless generations. And now - it sits sweating under an

Archivist's brow. And this brow looked up at me and

welcomed my presence, as it had always done. Without

needing another signal I entered the Archivist's personal

space. I watched in silence as the Archivist continued to

copy out his commentary; taking care to make each word

exact. It was crucial that all archives be correct, without

errors. Information for us is highly prized. You could say

that C-T thrives upon it. It is what maintains our power

centres, our systems and structures. Information is what

keeps us growing. The Lawgivers believe in progress

through information. The archivists collect and collate - yet

it is the Lawgivers who interpret and dictate. Information is

a commodity. In fact, it is more like a dark, thick blood that coagulates and congeals, as well as flows. I wonder if it is the static nature of information that now characterizes our civilization…the obsession with storage over renewal, of collection over development. I am wondering this as the Archivist beckoned me over with a conspirational smile. 'Do you know what this is, child of Johan?' I moved forward and looked at a block of information. The symbols were unfamiliar to me. I shook my head. 'This,' continued the Archivist, 'is the inventory of our trade here in C-T over the past eight passes of the two suns.' My face must have remained unimpressed. Yet the Archivist just chuckled and waved away my look with a swish of his hand.

'You may not be impressed. Yet what did you expect - a revelation?! The days of revelation are over. There are no more prophets, and thus no more great truths. We live in the afterburn of truths. We live in their shadow and must be grateful for this. Revelation is what brought us here -

stability is what will help us remain. What most people do not understand is that change can only come through established stability. If not, it manifests as chaos and not change. And chaos, child of Johan, is the beginning of the end.'

I walked over to the sealed door and touched its symbolic emblem. It was a sacred room. I could not enter. It was reserved for those of the Guild of Archivists. Behind the door lay an artificially chilled room that housed all the Archivist's information blocks. Here they would be protected from the dust and heat of C-T days. The contents of the room would be regularly transferred to the main storage facility at the Guild of Archivists. In this central location only guild elders and the Lawgivers are permitted to enter and retrieve the information. Local storage rooms are accessible to all C-T Archivists, such as

my father. I touched once again the emblem on the door
and traced its shape. To the sensation in my fingers it
represented something mysterious, beyond reach, and yet
something knowingly dead. There was an absence of life -
innate yet unmoving. Unable to move. Perhaps that was it;
this was the feeling I had when in the presence of the
friendly Archivist. It was a willingness mixed with an
inability. These two forces pulling at each other created a
balance - a centre that was static and yet secure. And within
this unmoving centre the Guild of Archivists maintained a
tradition, a ritualistic history that was as flat as it was linear.

'You may think that an inventory of our trade is of no use.
Yet it could be both our future and our past.' The Archivist
was leaning back in his chair as he eyed my interest in the
Guild door. 'You yourself know the power of information.
It creates - it makes existence. Without it we have nothing
to show. Imagine, if you can, some far distant future when

upon this planet of ours, C-T and our civilization exists no
more.' I tried to resist a smile. It was not a difficult thing to
imagine. Not in these recent days. 'A future civilization,
many sun cycles from now, may find these information
blocks of ours. To us, they may only be inventories, yet to
this future civilization they will be clues to our existence.
From this information they can learn of our society - our
language, structures, and systems. To them it will be a
revelation - and our civilization will live again in the minds
of others. We shall exist in another time, in another form.
This is the power of information - it carries like an eternal
vessel. It is like a code amongst the suns.'

The Archivist was becoming passionate now. I could see
his cheeks begin to turn a reddish hue as if his body was
diverting blood to these flesh sacks. Regardless of the
cause, it was refreshing to see the existence of passion -

even if it was a mental manifestation. I could imagine this
mental passion somehow also indirectly feeding his body;
thus adding further folds of flesh to his lugubrious belly.

'Maybe you wish for information to be more alive? I
remember you over many years, child of Johan. I have
observed your interest. You secretly desire information.
You chase it as an invisible hunter. Yet you cannot deny it.
You have grown up with it!' I was about to protest, yet
caught myself at the last moment. I chose not to react to
this. The Archivist was knowingly, and cleverly, attempting
to rouse me. His instinct about me was right; yet his
interpretation was incorrect. Archivists never develop their
interpretative faculty. Perhaps it would be dangerous if they
did. The Archivist raised his eyebrows at my lack of
response, and then rose from his chair. 'I see. It is not
information that you seek. It is something far truer that
attracts you. Maybe it is revelation after all?' Again I held

back any reaction. I wished for the Archivist to stimulate some interpretive sense rather than hand him information freely. 'Like I said before, my young friend - the days of revelation and prophets are over. It is well and truly over. The last person to call themselves a prophet in C-T was tied to a post where two avenues intersect.' My body gave an involuntary jerk. The Archivist noticed this. He paused. It was as if he were internally calculating the amount of information to retrieve. Perhaps weighing his actions against some future time? Archivists have a weakness in their attraction to legacy. I had first noticed this in my father. And this Archivist here was no exception. Legacy could be the single most precious thing in a civilization that strives for commonality and barren consensus. Here, the individuals were the mass; and the mass had one voice. One voice that was provided for them.

I followed the Archivist into a low room with bare walls. In

the middle of the room were a table and two chairs.

Alongside one wall was a small cupboard. The Archivist

gestured for me to sit as he opened the cupboard and

brought a dish to the table. The dish contained a heat-

baked sweet cake. The Archivist cut off two slices and

offered one to me. I accepted with grace and we both

began to quietly nibble the delicacy.

'I have information about the last prophet.' The Archivist

spoke in a hushed voice, as if worried our conversation

would be overheard. Like the room, the Archivist's tones

were low. 'There are records of him existing. This

information was taken out of public records, yet I have

seen the archive. I read it all. I remember being very

surprised at the time. I was a young archivist then, and I

had to be immaculate in my work. I could speak of this

assignment to no one. Over the years the memory of this

prophet has returned to my mind on occasion. Yet I quickly put it away - file it to the deep recesses of my mind. There is nothing I can do with this information. Another strange thing is that this information is ambiguous.' I looked askew at the Archivist as he munched the last of his sweet cake. 'Yes, that was a double reason for it to be strange to me. It was not constant fact. The information kept changing. This man was sometimes referred to as a prophet, at other times a madman. It was recorded that this man...this prophet, madman, or whatever...that he caused great disturbance by his words. He would wander the avenues shouting and declaring his revelation for all to hear! Which family he came from I do not know. This information has been permanently deleted from the records. Perhaps it was from shame...or?' The Archivist pulled himself back, as if considering the gravity of his own revelation to me. Yet I urged him to go on. I knew it would be this moment or never. One must never lose the energy of an opportune moment.

'This madman used to walk the avenues on either side of the Citadel declaring that we - all the people - are light beings dressed in rags of flesh. He used to shout out that just as there are light beings within the Citadel, in the flesh of stone, there are light beings within us - those of human flesh. We are of the same family. And some people began to listen to him. It was these people that started to refer to the madman as a prophet. The records also mention his clothes. This man did not wear the general clothes like the rest of us in C-T. He somehow had managed to make his own design - his own colours. The records say he was dressed in clothes that were patches of different colours. Incredible, isn't it?!' I nodded in agreement; although the core of my being was in a different form of agreement...a different alignment. This was indeed new information for me.

'This man must have been like a whole new breed!' The Archivist whistled through his teeth and shook his head. 'Imagine a person like that walking the streets today? Wearing his own clothes, all these odd and fancy colours patched together. Talk about leaving behind the crowd! Today such a person would quickly be grabbed and exiled to the outer limits of the sun mutants. But back then - who knows? It must have come as a shock to everyone in C-T. I think it was the first time. The archives have no record of any other similar occurrence. Well, none that I can find...unless another lone archivist in C-T has other information like mine not shared.'

Saying this, the Archivist looked up at me and read my expression clearly. 'No, we archivists don't share everything, contrary to what some others may think. In fact, we share very little. It is forbidden. We share our experiences - and some of our crazy ideas!' said the Archivist with a suppressed giggle. 'Yet we rarely share the details, the facts of our own archiving. It is not accepted by the Guild. We work so much alone. We work for the love and care of the information. We are like slaves to this information. For us it is our equivalent of knowledge. It is the only knowledge we know.' Again, the Archivist clearly read my own expression. 'Yes, perhaps information is the only knowledge our civilization has.'

The room lapsed into silence as we both sat with our thoughts. Was there significance to this long ago isolated event? Could there today be some trace, some tangible effect, now playing out from the past antics of this madman? The Archivist began tapping his fingers against the table. I knew he had more to tell me, so I gave him an urging look.

'It must have been quite a sight! This madman strolling the streets and avenues in his fancy garb and declaring to all of C-T that we are true light beings! Yet, you know, this is not the worst that could be said. Is it not a positive attribute? This message could most certainly have brought hope to many people. It was not like he was calling for an overthrow of the C-T elders, or a revolution against the Lawgivers. So why the big fuss?' The Archivist turned behind him to peek out of the low window. 'Mmm…it is soon time for our midday enclosure. The two suns are close to their zenith now. I must secure this place.' The Archivist rose from the table and secured the iron plate across the window. He then left the room to secure the rest of the dwelling. The low room I was in now felt like a place of containment. It felt like a micro-scale C-T. We live in such close confinement. And yet not only physically. Our very ideas are managed through the minimalism of our movements. Being constrained to the shadows of the Citadel walls could have released us to roam in other ways. Our minds could have sought grander solutions to what we as yet do not know. Yet the shadows have given us greater fear rather than release. We live huddled in rooms. C-T life scuttles around in trade, in storage, in commonality. Yet once, it now appears, there was one person who stood out colourfully from the masses and made a statement that pierced to our depths. We were forced to ask and question ourselves - what type of *being* are we? It was a madman. A madman to the sane - and a prophet to the half-insane.

The Archivist stepped back into the room; his brow now fully plated with a surface of sweat. 'We must soon leave. The avenue will be gaining its suns shortly. Let us be inside our homes until the two suns fall and darkness brings us

out again. Why not share this resting time with our family -

we would be happy to facilitate your rest with us?' I knew

the Archivist's offer was a genuine one. And I knew his

family also to be gentle in their receiving of guests. Yet now

was not the time to adhere to rest, or to succumb to social

C-T ritual. I felt unfinished in my task; incomplete in my

need. I shook my head gently.

As we were leaving I gently touched the Archivist on his

elbow. It was just a light touch. A touch of camaraderie - as

if to acknowledge and thank him for the information he

had kindly shared with me. He needn't have shared

anything; and he knew it. He always knew it - it was his

function. The Archivist's rounded face looked at me. I saw

a look of gratitude and sadness at the same time. It was a

mix of below-surface emotions that punctured just slightly

beneath the skin. A momentary tinge swept across his cheeks.

'I don't know what happened to the madman, this prophet. All records cf his coming - and his going - have been erased. He seems to have been an anomaly…an anomaly of colour withir a world of shadow.'

We both parted on the avenue with a smile and a wave. It was a genial parting, where less is more.

Chapter Six - The Avenue

The avenue on our side of the Citadel was entering the rest period. The two suns were close to their zenith and the shadows from the Citadel wall were thin. Whilst one part of C-T rested another part would awaken. Our civilization not only nestles in the shadows of walls but also within the movements of two suns. In the midst of these great natural forces a flicker of human civilization had grown its dependency. There are those amongst us in C-T that still believes in the superiority of humanity. It is humanity, they say, that will engineer the future of this planet - and to design our way into and amongst the stars. Yet such designs, such thinking, are the product of blindness. Our blindness is like a disease. Not a disease that stops us from seeing what is in front of us. It is a disease that shuts us off from the bigger picture. This disease creates for humans a sense of reality that is separate, cut-off, and isolated. It is a disease that stops us from looking up at the sky each day. For if we were to look up, and truly see, we would know without doubt that we are bound to the fate of the two suns - and thus all the stars.

I fear that C-T is already too heavily infected. When we are blind we do not notice the encroaching permanence of shadows. We need both the light and the dark to survive. These changing energies give us our momentum. If there were but one, we would perish through stagnation. The Citadel is a gift that shows us this truth every day as she dissects and delivers this interplay of light and shadow. And so this is the pendulum swing of C-T, like two hemispheres in balance.

I have become more restless lately. I wonder if, as the
Archivist suggested, such manifestations are an anomaly?
Or are such things a reflection of what we understand as
normal? My mind is too active now to be falsely subdued
into rest. If I wish to remain outdoors then I must
circumvent my way closely along the Citadel walls to reach
the parallel avenue. The shadows on the other side will
have already arisen and now be fully upon those dwellings.
Trade and commerce will soon commence.

I am not alone as I make my way between the two principle
avenues, keeping close to the Citadel walls. There are
always shreds of movement at this time as people hurry to
finalize their tasks. Filaments of activity dart amongst the
shadows. There are those who live more permanently
within the shadows; who forfeit their rest period, their time
for enclosure. There are functions that still need to be

done. Those of us that pass upon the shadowed streets
rarely acknowledge each other. We pass silently as bodies in
retreat. Only those we are close to, or are family, spare time
for a cordial greeting. We move with sure footing; not so
that we do not fall, but so as not to touch. The shadows of
the Citadel walls may give us shelter, yet they do not hide
us.

I move along the intersecting avenue that joins the parallel
principle avenues. This side of the Citadel is a
thoroughfare, a passage. On this side of the wall people
seldom stop. There are fewer dwellings here because of the
increased exposure to the passing of the two suns. There
are storage facilities and general secondary buildings. This
is a transitory avenue; no-one in C-T lingers here long. That
is why there is always the fast patter of feet upon these
streets. And all those who pass huddle close to the Citadel

wall. It is here, on this zenith of the passing two suns, that I see her approach.

She is the daughter of our local health provider. Her father represents our sector of C-T and belongs to the Guild of Medics. Her father is intelligent and caring. I remember visiting him many times, often to check my throat and vocal chords. His remedies are standard, as are all the health providers; yet his manner and composure is softer. That is where I first saw her, his daughter. I noticed how soft she was too in her mannerisms and behaviour. Upon first seeing her I felt a freshness not normally encountered amongst C-T. Her young enquiring eyes seemed to soak in the environment without reaction or judgement. I noticed all this quietly. That is how I know things - I observe. For a long time now I have been observing the world around me. I see life in C-T as a large stellar ship slowing down. There is no more acceleration; no more thrust. The large ship now only cruises upon its past momentum. Eventually it must come to rest. Yet because it still moves, its gradual deceleration is imperceptible to most. The present sense of movement placates the minds of all those who live and survive within this momentum. The mind cannot conceive of a far future moment when the whole of existence comes to a rest. We continue to move, and yet we are slowing down.

I hope, and urge within me, that the young ones will feel this. They are the future of C-T. The health provider's daughter is amongst these young ones. In her I see only potential. In her approach I notice her active observation. In her gait I sense something unusual. It is...what we would call *harmony*. This is a strange concept; yet I sense this when I see her conduct. This *harmony* is when someone connects with something innate and everlasting. Perhaps it is a connection with something that we've always known. Like the Citadel - we have always known it. We all grew up within sight of its walls, within its shadows. And yet we do not know how to reach out to it.

As she passes near to me the health provider's daughter gives the tiniest smile of recognition. In return I give a slight nod of my head. It is such an almost imperceptible connection, and yet so powerful. We are breaking boundaries here. In this micro-moment a touch of warmth passed between us. An imagery of thought enters my head suddenly. What if everyone in C-T connected like this? What would C-T be like if such connection became the norm? It was almost too impossible - too unbearable - to imagine. Perhaps in this lay the future...the only possible future.

As a civilization on this rock in space we are connected to everything that happens amongst the stars above. We must no longer be isolated. We must no longer think of ourselves as unique; or as an accident. Otherwise why is the Citadel here? She is like a living star. Here to connect us - to the stars and to ourselves. I am sure the Citadel is in more places than here...like a bridge, a contact, there is meaning written into her indelible stone. I then slow down my pace...it comes to my mind suddenly - but is it stone? I stop to face the Citadel wall that looms like a monolith into the half sun-seared sky. To us it has always been stone - stone in our stories, in our history, in our sight. It has become completely set as stone within our minds. Yet what is such stone? With a struggling new mind I reach out my hand to touch against the lean verticality of the Citadel. With a shock surprise I find that it feels cold to my touch.

And it is so smooth; so unlike the stone walls of my mind. I peer close to look. There are no cracks, or lines; nothing to mark the joining of stone pieces. No - this could not be one complete stone. Impossible! And yet how could it have been constructed? It is an impenetrable wall; there are no ways to climb its smooth surface. I take out a metal trade token I have in my pocket and scratch it against the wall. I push hard against the smooth surface, and yet I am unable to make the slightest mark. I look up and follow the Citadel wall as it disappears into the far sky. I see a huge inhuman hand reaching for the centre of the stars. I - we - are out of our depth. Our civilization is but a tiny flicker of struggling life amongst the immensity of existence. Yet within this unsettling thought lies a kernel of hope and untraceable joy.

I arrive at the main avenue that extends from the other side of the Citadel. I am approaching the other split-side of C-T.

Still, it is familiar to me. I visit both sides often, making use of my time between studies. The colour of the sky above me is a mixed hue of light and shadow. The two suns have now passed over the Citadel. The air remains warm and dry; there is heat upon my face yet it is indirect and dispersed. It is heat from the morning as the suns fell on this side of C-T. The exposed streets still retain their warmth. It is a hot day, dusty and arid, and the shadows from the wall are a home to us.

Across the street I see the dwelling of the Scholar - his door open to welcome the new shadowed day.

Chapter Seven - The Scholar

In recent times I have come less regularly to visit the
Scholar. He is getting old now, and a young apprentice sits
by him to assist and learn. In my younger years I was
allotted a part of my time to learn from the scholar's
classes. Those of my quarter of C-T were assigned our
times for visitation. I was intrigued by such thoughts back
then; the words entered me and became as ropes to climb
forward. Often I would return and communicate with the
scholar in my free time. I remember being impressed by the
Scholar's certainty. It was as if he knew everything in its
place - no uncertainty or vague unknowns. This certainty
gave the Scholar an air of authority that dissolved any
doubts. For me, that words could exist in such certainty
was a new discovery. So I returned many times to learn of
this certainty. In the end, perhaps it was inevitable that I
would discover the shadow side to this - that such certainty

created its own uncertainty. It was then that the veneer blurred and became unclear for me.

'Ah, the inquisitive Student. It is good to see you back.' The Scholar raised his head from the desk and squinted through his eye receptacles. He had grown thinner in the face since our last meeting. He still had his tuft of white hair cut short upon his head, yet now supported by a gaunt face. For such a long time this man had helped C-T to create its learning texts and ideas. He was one of several, who all belonged to the Guild of Scholars. And now as he had reached his final fifth of life he was training a new body to step into his function. This younger man was not much older than myself, yet he seemed to have practiced well the serious face of a scholar. Both the men, old and young, bore expressions devoid of muscle movement. They held faces of certainty; perhaps as security against their own battle with an uncertain universe.

I nodded and smiled to both men. I was genuinely glad to be back in the Scholar's dwelling. It was now, from the old Scholar's face, that I could mark the rapid passage of time. Ideas could not hold back the destiny of man's demise, despite the vigour of their fight. Nor too could ideas stem the onslaught of a future whose coming is known regardless of all events. And yet the Guild of Scholars were determined in their bid to promote rigid study and learning as the pinnacle of C-T. Every guild, in its own way, fights for prominence and power in a civilization where both are fleeting.

'We are just finishing our latest study,' announced the Scholar as he folded his hands upon the desk. 'My apprentice here is learning well his new life trade.' The apprentice acknowledged me with the slightest of glances, as if afraid of forfeiting a moment of concentration. 'It is a project that has taken us many suns to prepare - and rightly so, for it is connected with the very suns above our heads. Indeed, with those very suns that have helped us to understand life and reality on this planet of ours.' The Scholar was observant enough to note my moment of hesitation. 'Ah, you are quick to question how I define reality. I remember this as being one of your weak spots. It seems you have retained this dilemma in your mind.' I said nothing, not wishing to be drawn into a debate within his own territory. It was true that I cared not for the Scholar's physical descriptions of reality; yet for now I wished to listen to more.

'Our reality here on this planet,' continued the Scholar, 'is defined by our biology. This in turn is defined by our two suns. We are given heat and light from the two suns, both now and as then during the Forming.' I sighed internally. Yes - the Forming! How well we all knew of the Forming. From our earliest days we had been taught the Forming, so we knew well our beginnings. The Forming taught us how life started on this planet - how we came to be. By the grace of the starry heavens we were a glorious accident. The rays of the two suns shone down upon this bare planet and spliced with the minerals. Early organic minerals were produced that, over time, *formed* into living cells through the heat of the two suns. It took aeons of untold time before the earliest legless land animals were finally *formed.* And more aeons still until such land slugs finally morphed into the human being we have today. This is the Forming. So simple, so logical...and so anaemic to life. Yet this is the official story. We human beings are an accident within the grander accident of cosmic life. It is an accident that the two suns provide our warmth, nutrients, and energy for living. It is an accident that the Citadel stands here amongst us as our shelter and saviour. And it is the greatest accident that we humans now have minds to contemplate these things. For all that we are unable to fully comprehend, the Forming provides its own shelter for us and keeps us safe from our unknowing. We here in C-T strive to find answers to what we do not understand, even if we do not understand the answers we tell ourselves. The Scholars, in their function, explain to us how we can understand these ideas. And this gives them their power.

'And as the two suns gave us our Forming, so they dictate our movements. And how are our movements calculated?' It was a rhetorical question, and yet still the Scholar paused; for effect, not reply. 'Our movements comply according to the shadows that form across C-T. And the major cause of our shadows is the Citadel. For all the cycles of the two suns that have passed us in C-T, we have yet to calculate, with true research, the angles of the shadows at each moment upon our day. So this, in simple speech, is the essence of our project which now nears completion. Come Student!' The Scholar stood up and marched out of the room. Despite his frail condition he still exerted the outward force of a person fully capable of his function. Such necessities, perhaps, are hard to lose; if even permitted. Yet when once I smiled inwardly at being called Student, now it made my stomach constrict.

The research room was a restrained combination of order and dishevelment. That everything was in its place I did not doubt. Where that place was, and in which order, was known only to the Scholar. Good luck to the new apprentice who had to learn such ways by being *in presence* only. There is much that is taught by exact procedure. There is a greater amount that can only be absorbed by

being in the presence of a teacher - by observing through
the mind and body. I too have learnt much by being *in*
presence with many people. It has helped me to unfold my
path into the future.

'Here are some of our measurements.' The Scholar brought
some information blocks over to the large table that
dominated the room. He spread them out and ran his
hands over their markings. Often such gestures can say
more than words. The body movements, the twitches, the
touches; they reveal a language all of their own. I know for
I have observed them all my life. I had to learn *in presence*
the silent language that communicates between all people,
all things. In the Scholar's hands I read the presence of
precision; the production of dry logic. Here was something
real to him. These calculations, these collected facts,
represented what was real about the world. It was these tiny
artefacts that constructed the life of security, of certainty.

'The regular and gradual shifts of the shadows from the Citadel walls form the schedule of C-T life. Our lives are governed by the ascendance and descent of these shadows. We can say that our culture, its forms and structures, are a direct result of the path of these shadows. By knowing more about the time path of these shadows we can discern the origins of cultural behaviour.'

I reached over and gently rested my fingers upon the information board. I ran my fingers across the symbolic Citadel and further up toward the two suns. My fingers eventually came to the edge of the board; and I purposely continued until my hand was upon the table.

'We do not have interest in the stars.' The Scholar's tone was decisive and curt. 'What affects us here and now are the movements of shadows. We know these are caused by

the two suns, obviously. What? Ah yes, and by the Citadel.
Yet what lies beyond the two suns, or exists up there with
our suns, is not a direct part of our life here. Nor even are
we interested in what *is* the Citadel. For us it is a building.
And this building has a central function of providing us
with shadow. How the building came to be…well, that is
left for loose minds with much to think on. Have you been
up to the Citadel, and touched it?' I nodded that I had.
'Good. So you will know that it is hard, and real to the
touch. It is not a phantasm, nor a myth. It is a real, tangible
building. That is our reality here in C-T. Trust in the
building - do not research ephemeral ideas about unknown
light and what is beyond the stars. Only what you know can
be real to you. If you do not know a thing then it lies in
your imagination. Was our civilization ever based on
imagination? No. It was concrete understanding and
knowing that created practical application. There is no
greater truth than the discoveries we can make from fact.'

The Scholar's eye receptacles had slipped down his nose as he spoke. He now inched them back up with a point of his finger.

The Scholar was in a mood to talk and share on this occasion. On other occasions he had been more withdrawn and not wishing for any distraction. Now that his project was coming to its close he seemed eager to discuss his own thinking with me. The Scholar pulled some sheaths down from their shelf and spread them on the table. 'Here,' he said, pointing at some diagrammatic design. 'Here is the C-T plan. See how the quarters are built in exact relation and distance from the Citadel? First the planning was random. The first inhabitants made dwellings under the walls without thought for expansion. The later waves started here, behind the first dwellings, and are much more structured in their positions. As the dwellings reach further back they start to thin at the centre, for here the first rays

of the sun emerge. You see how people's lives are

measured?' I understood what the Scholar wanted to say:

that human lives need to be measured. But not only

measured - they need management. 'You realize now,

Student, that nothing here in C-T is an accident other than

the Forming. Humans have created their own order out of

the cosmic disorder. This is our great achievement. And

perhaps we are alone in this.'

I stepped back from the table. It was now that I realized

how small the room actually was. It had always seemed

much larger to me; full of research and study. Now, as the

two of us were alone, it suddenly felt confining. Before I

could answer, the Scholar wagged his finger at me. 'You

must accept the fact that human civilization is alone. Since

the Forming was a random accident, it is almost impossible

that the exact same conditions will apply on another planet.

In this respect we are unique, yet also very alone. Humanity

is unlikely to have any relation with the universe - only with

this planet. What we do here applies to us, and us alone. So

we must be precise, and calculate what is in our best

interests. We must manage our present so that we have a

future made for us. We may not be able to control the

passage of the two suns, or the movements in the skies, yet

everything here on this planet is our domain. In this

isolation we must socially manage civilization according to

strict guidelines. If not, then we are in danger of falling into

the chaos that is randomness.'

The Scholar paused in breath and began to pace across the

room. I had the sensation that he was talking more to

himself now than to me. This is perhaps the truer function

of the student; to assist the Scholar in knowing more about

his own thoughts than in the communication of them. 'And randomness is where progress begins to falter. This is the first step to the dissolution of society. Creativity was a part of the Forming, yet order and management is what sustains a project for the long-term. People need to be managed. In fact, it is what they actually want whether they state it or not. Without adequate order people become bored, restless. They do not have sufficient intelligence to create meaning for themselves, so they seek order and balance. We scholars know this - the Guild has always known this. We consider this part of our duty, which we take seriously. You may frown, Student, yet this is surely the case. Yes, people fear freedom, and do not know how to handle such liberty. Their liberty must be constrained by adapting it into a social order that becomes their life. The Lawgivers fulfil their function in providing the guidance by their laws. Yet this is only a skeleton, a structure - it is not the flesh of society.' The Scholar held both his arms out to the side with his palms facing up. 'On one hand we Scholars educate the Students of C-T. We teach our people in learning and understanding. This means we need to research the things of this world, and calculate how matter operates. And with the other hand we study human behaviour. We learn how to map human life and from this we create social management. Our understanding filters into law, as well as into trade, and family life. Human life only *appears* random. In truth it is highly patterned, and quite regular. We are creatures, creatures who think - nothing more. Just like the cycles of the suns we have our fixed routines also. We have our standard movements, our daily events that connect us to the passing of the shadows. We live within these patterns - within these shadows.'

The Scholar walked away from the table. He signalled for me to follow him as he left the room and exited the dwelling place. We both stood outside under the warm shadow of the Citadel wall on the parallel side of C-T. I say parallel as my family dwelling place - my quarter – lay on the other side. Those of us from my side refer to here as the parallel. I am sure those people dwelling here say the same about us. The official name for this side of C-T is Rise C-T; and my side is called Fall C-T. These names reflect the movement of the two suns. I turned to observe the Scholar as he stared solidly at the Citadel. For a brief moment both appeared as rigid as each other. And yet I sensed no understanding between them: no connection, no communication. The Scholar pointed out to where the Citadel stood. 'That huge structure there is a fact. We don't know its origins. Neither can we discover the source of its internal lights, nor why they shine continuously without ever dimming. This we may never know. It has eluded us until now. Perhaps it is an energy source - or something else entirely. We have almost given up the desire to know.

This rock sculpture is impenetrable to our research. Its

doors are locked to us. That, of course, is a false statement

since the Citadel has no doors. So we study what is. We do

not study what is not.' The Scholar turned his glance

sideways to meet mine. 'You should understand that,

Student, being the child of Johan. You should appreciate

regularity and order. Why do you waste your thoughts on

the sun mutants who live outside of C-T?'

The Scholar had remembered my earlier interest. I

wondered why he would remember such a thing - did he

consider it an oddity? An anomaly perhaps?

'I knew immediately you were not a person suited to a

scholarly approach to life. Although your mind is bright,

and has potential, you lack the ability to focus on the real.

A scholarly mind must focus on learning to understand

what is right before us. It must focus on that which is

useful, and which has a function. These so-called sun mutants are no longer a part of our humanity. They have branched away from us. They have devolved. They are primitive. Their skins must be so dark now, burnt from the sun. They do not have an orderly society like we do in C-T. They will not make progress. They are stagnating. They will die out soon. Yet C-T will grow from strength to strength. It has a future. Any why? Because we have conquered what is unnatural to us, and we have tamed this. We have organized the randomness into structure and meaning. We have skeleton and we have flesh. We have order and understanding. And we store this information. We retain that which is useful to us. We do not dance in the sand like the sun mutants. We in C-T understand our reality. And you must too, Student. Our reality is here, amongst the solid things in life - not amid the star dust!' The Scholar turned to walk back into his dwelling. Then he suddenly stopped, as if a thought had hit him.

'Student. I know you are young. Ones like you must be the future of C-T for us. My project must benefit you - all of you. We are all together - we are all the same. Think on this, and help to benefit C-T.' The Scholar stepped back into the shadowed rooms of his research. I remained. The great Citadel moored across from me. It had witnessed this exchange…No, *she* had witnessed this exchange. Although the Scholar had spoken, I had felt no communication in his exchange. They had been words devoid of touch. Words of structure, yet not the words of meaning that he had emphasized upon so much. Yet what did I know - I was only Student?

The Citadel had not reached out to the Scholar - nor the Scholar to her. The world of the intangible was more than a shadow to the Scholar's mind. Only the solid tangibles could fit intc his space. For me, it was a restricted world.

Not the world of the future. Not the world of any future.

The tangibles are only a stage, I feel. A stage we must

overcome...or stagnate.

Rise C-T was fully in shadow now and I could move freely

along its avenues. Busyness once again came to C-T as

various trades, meetings, and encounters enacted their day.

Not far from where I stood a great commotion was

underway. I moved in that direction.

Chapter Eight - The Tokener

Several people had gathered outside of the dwelling of a money lender, known in C-T as a Tokener. There was an argument between several men, one of whom I recognized to be the Tokener. This is not a rare thing to see - an argument in C-T. This is to be expected when there is so much trade going on in such a relatively small area. Sometimes there are arguments between people from Rise C-T and those from Fall C-T. It seems that even though we are of one C-T there are still trifling territorial divides. Disputes are a product of human nature, as far as I can tell. They also arise from boredom, and the need for conflict and tension in what, for many people, are monotonous lives. This is also why there are regular public debates in C-T. Even by listening to debate and disputation people find they are able to relieve themselves of tension. That is why arguments more often than not attract eager witnesses.

The dwelling of the Tokener was in my line of direction. I had not intended to visit the Tokener as it is not a trade that interests me. I have always found Tokeners in C-T to be guarded people. You could say anti-social, if such a thing is possible in C-T. I recognize that their trade is required, yet it appears to attract a particular type of person. Still, one can never be completely sure of anything in C-T. Despite its ordered functioning, there are many things that must align themselves with necessity. And a person can never be sure what that necessity may be, or how it may cross their path in C-T life.

A tall man, thin and of light build, was arguing forcibly with the Tokener. The tall man had to bend his neck to engage with the Tokener, who by comparison was his opposite.

This particular Tokener was a person of lesser growth - what we call a *dharfid*. Dharfids, because of their delayed growth, are of short height. Their bodies are often proportional, like the rest of us; just that they are short in stature. This condition does not affect their minds or intelligence, as was noted by this Tokener who was quick to respond to the thin man's accusations.

'You have been disgraced by your word. You promised that my credit was good and would not be requested paid back until at least the third new cycle of the two suns. You are not a Tokener of your word.' The thin man was shaking his finger at the Tokener. This scene was strangely reminiscent of a father berating his child, proportionally speaking. Yet the Tokener, despite his size, projected the appearance of a more mature person. Perhaps this was helped by his heavily dark bearded face, upon which he wore strong-rimmed eye receptacles.

'I gave you my word according to law given to all Tokeners. Your credit was guaranteed by the Guild of Tokeners. Our deal was perfectly legitimate and correct.'

'Then why has my credit been requested to be paid back in full. I'm not ready for this!'

'This is a matter of a greater law - the law of C-T,' replied the Tokener with a secure calmness. It was immediately obvious to my eye that the Tokener knew his position was firmly supported by law. A Tokener always has this protection. That is why all Tokeners must act according to both the laws of their guild and the law as given by the Lawgivers of C-T. In this way, they never enter into disputes as a personal matter. It is always the fault of the law! So Tokeners are never to blame - they are merely facilitators within the law. They allow the transmission and facilitation of credit. They are responsible for its flow - and its stoppage. C-T life depends upon the careful maintenance of this flow. Credit is the energy of our civilization. It is both a physical flow, and yet often it can operate on the back of a word, or a gesture. Credit for us stands as an indispensable tangible and intangible force.

'What do you mean by greater law? Are you playing with me dharfid?' The Tokener knew he was being insulted, yet he did not show this.

'The greater law of C-T is under the Lawgivers. I promised you the credit under the protection of the Guild of Tokeners. By law after two new cycles of the two suns all credit transactions are under the ruling authority of C-T law. That is, under the Lawgivers. They can choose to request credit to be returned if they feel it can be put to better use in other C-T related projects. Your case was examined and the request for credit return was issued by a central Lawgiver. The Guild of Tokeners promised that it would not ask for credit return before at least the third cycle of the two suns. And that remains so - *we* are not asking for your credit. The Lawgivers of C-T demand its return for their purposes. And our guild must abide by this overruling decision. You do not have a dispute with us. It is with the Law.' The thin man threw up his arms at this. I could see the desperation in his voice and behaviour. This credit must be critical to him. Flanking the thin man was a similar sized man, who I presumed from his looks to be a brother. Families are discouraged from collectively entering disputes. It is expected that the individual shall deal with any such issues. The brother was present for support, yet did not say anything. He only shook his head. He knew the law could not be overruled.

'Yet why did you not state this other law before?!'

'It is infrequently applied. We cannot be expected to state every law of the Lawgivers. They can overrule us when they choose. We too are at their mercy. We are citizens of C-T the same as you. We are under the same conditions. Do not take this personally.'

'How am I supposed to take it?! You were too quick to offer me credit. I hardly heard a breath escape from your mouth.'

'We Tokeners do breathe, believe me,' answered the Tokener with a tone of irony.

'Well, that surprises me! In one breath you can make a multitude of transactions. You are too easy in offering your credit, and too quick to escape trouble and blame. You hide behind your laws, and all the so-called greater laws. And nothing sticks to you, does it Tokener?'

'That does not stick where there is no cause for anything to stick.' The Tokener had maintained a flat, expressionless face throughout the exchange. He offered no assistance, and no further explanation.

'This is your greed that has done this. Nothing but your greed!'

'How so?' The Tokener's emotionless responses were aggravating the thin man. His anger was finding no accepting recipient. The Tokener was refusing to step into

the same energetic sphere. I could see this lack of

connection was frustrating the aggrieved man.

'How so? How so! Because you, and those like you, do not

wish to consider the consequences of your actions. Your

only desire is to accumulate. And we, normal people like us,

we are only of use to you when we help you to accumulate.

When we are in trouble you cast us aside and take back

from our bones.'

'We only take back what is lawfully ours. We deal only with

those people who are mature enough to understand the

consequences of their own actions. We defend our trade

for the good of C-T. It is not in our remit to defend your

moral sensibility, or lack of such. You must deal with your

own circumstances. And we Tokeners shall continue to

operate within the regulated jurisdiction of the Lawgivers.

Any argument you have you may take to them. Your issue

is now with the Lawgivers. Your contract with the Guild of

Tokeners is now terminated. And now it is time that we parted.'

The Tokener gave a curt nod and withdrew inside his trade dwelling. The thin man raised his fist silently into the air. It was an empty gesture that the small crowd of people recognized and sympathized with. Anything else now was futile. The matter was closed, and framed within the jurisdiction of law. It was an efficient and effective way of putting the thin man's dispute beyond reach. Authority had quashed a personal grievance into a vacuum. The Tokener's trade is the most highly protected in C-T by the Lawgivers. All disputes in the transaction of credit are referred to the Lawgivers. It is used as a shield by the Guild of Tokeners, and offers them a free license to operate agreements many consider dubious. By the same hand, the Lawgivers are strengthened by their regulatory power over the trade of credit. Their ability to call in bad credit feeds their own

accumulative wants. It also feeds their status. I remember

one time my father commenting that credit was once about

circulation, and that now it was about accumulation. And

when credit is accumulated like information, he said, then it

loses its energy and serves the few instead of the many. I

am beginning to feel that he is right.

The small crowd around the thin man had now dispersed.

The only figure remaining with the thin man was the one I

suspected to be his brother. Their looks reflected a

weariness; a knowledge of defeat. I felt a deep sadness

emanate from their faces. The human face - so expressive!

It holds a wealth of unspoken communication in C-T

where daily communication is vocal and yet expressionless.

Like lost souls stranded after a storm the two men sulked

slowly away down the avenue.

I walked over to the entrance of the Tokener's dwelling and peered inside. I saw a well-organized room with walls covered in storage space and artefacts for storing content. It did not look welcoming. Nor did I have any intention to enter. I knew that, usually, for a person to visit the Tokener an agreed meeting time is required. I stepped back outside. I leant against the side of the dwelling and stared at the colossal Citadel in front of me. It gave me the sensation that all of our human grievances, sufferings, and struggles are as dust against the truth of this ageless monument. Our worries and petty divisions are but the playthings of scarabs that scuttle in the shadows. C-T and its residents are caught up within their distracting affairs that constitute life - whilst the Citadel stands motionless in the centre of it all. Its stillness is a lesson to behold. The Citadel does not abide by blind behaviour. It observes...and waits. I sensed that the Citadel was waiting for something - some moment,

some time. Perhaps it waits for something from us. For us

to indicate that we are ready. Yet ready for what?

'It is a blessing is it not?' I turned to see the Tokener

standing beside me at the door of his dwelling. In my

reverie I had not noticed his appearance. He was likewise

gazing in front of him, at the source of our shadows. I did

not reply. It was not a question he was posing. It was a

recognition. For a brief instant it felt as if we shared some

essence from the Citadel. Then the Tokener quickly broke

this fleeting connection, as if he feared its resonance.

'A blessing that we have this building to provide our

shadows,' said the Tokener matter-of-factly. 'Everything

finds its purpose eventually…even a building as mysterious

as this one. This huge thing, just standing there for as long

as anyone can remember - a building that no one goes in

and no one comes out of. It is more like a rock…a dead

rock. Yet here it is, providing us with all the shadows we need.' The Tokener saw that I was about to protest. 'Ah yes, there are those odd lights up there at the top. So I suppose it is not quite a dead rock. But why else is it here? While it's almost as good as lifeless it does supply us with a good life I suppose. You know, I sometimes think of this Citadel like a giant authority structure with its shadows watching over us. Maybe these grand shadows are its huge eyes and ears - knowing and recording all that we do and say. Like the rule of the Lawgivers we are unable to escape its jurisdiction. It's such an unmoving thing, don't you think?'

I observed the Tokener as he stood beside me, his neck craned up at the Citadel. He was smaller than I was; a dharfid body fully proportioned with strong arms. It seemed a little strange to me that such a person would powerfully regulate the circulation of so much of C-T's token trade. No, it was not strange. That is not the right word. I don't think we have the word for it, when there is a contrast in the reality of a situation. Perhaps I should invent a word for this. In a way the Tokener was right when he said that the Citadel is such an unmoving thing. Yet it allows for movement in C-T; movement and trade within its shadows. And the trade with the greatest movement is that of tokens and their credit. It is like the blood of C-T - within the flesh of shadows and bone of Citadel. This huge edifice facilitates all this movement and flow within C-T. It even allows for the existence of C-T. And so far it has asked for nothing in return. We do not even clean it or maintain it. It seems to maintain itself. Its smooth walls never appear to get damaged from the natural elements. I have never seen any visible cracks. I don't think we even know what it is made of. We just accept its presence - always and constantly in our lives.

The Tokener was fiddling with something small in his hands. When I turned to look he grinned at me and showed me his small symmetrical token.

'It's all about this. This is what creates movement and change. This is what keeps things going. Not anything else in C-T - certainly not its laws! The reality is that we must pay in life. There's no other truth. We are here on this planet. This is our existence. I am a dharfid, and that is my existence. Our civilization must keep moving - it must grow. What we have here as tokens is the energy of our civilization. Call it what you will, but these are just symbols. They are emblems, tokens for a larger reality...the reality of keeping human civilization together. And the Guild of Tokeners has the responsibility to oversee this duty and guard against its corruption. The Lawgivers may talk and talk about this and that. Yet there would be no keeping of the laws if there was no circulation of tokens. Mark me on that. I know of what I speak. Every civilization needs energy to sustain it. Ours is the energy of tokens for it is the energy of exchange.' As if on cue we both exchanged a glance. The Tokener's grinning face, taut with struggling expression, seemed to be in contrast to my calm, inquisitive look. The Tokener laughed and nodded his head. It was then that I noted that his head appeared to be quite large for his body; with a wide sloping forehead. He continued to nod his head, as if pushing his own thoughts through his mind.

'Some people say it's greed that controls the token trade. But I disagree. Real greed lies in people. People are greedy for comfort, for security. They don't want freedom, or truth - whatever that is! They greed after a happy and stress free life. That's why they let others control them. Control them through laws, or through tokens. Theirs is the greed of insecurity. And this weakness within people is what our human civilization is based on. The whole thing is based on greed - a greed within people that they feed with excuses. My function in the trade of tokens is not greed - I tell you this now! What I do is keep the peace. Keep the stability. I keep everyone's greed in working order!' The Tokener snorted and slapped his hands together. He looked like a person who had just discovered the inner secrets of our species, and was proud of his discovery. 'Well, I must go and keep our world in order. Someone has to! Good shadow time to you.' The Tokener raised his hand in a farewell gesture and disappeared back into his trade dwelling. Yet his parting gesture, I felt, had not really been for me. He had not even given me a final glance either. The last thing he looked at, and to where he raised his hand, was the Citadel.

I now had the impression that his whole talk had not really been for me. It had been for the Citadel, as if he knew it was listening to him. He had acknowledged its role as the grand observing authority. He had spoken for *her*. Was he attempting to give reason for his behaviour; or perhaps for *our* behaviour? Was he trying to justify human nature to the Citadel? Yet it was human nature as seen through the eyes of a Tokener - through just one Tokener. And I did not feel he was right. There is greed within some people...but so much more besides. When you look for the worst you only see the worst. It's true that C-T is a product of us. Yet it is also the product of other factors too - external ones. Just as we too are shaped by external things. Nothing, it seems to me, is from one thing only. Everything connects - it must do. I guess perspectives are all we have...

I continued to stroll down the Avenue. Everything we do, I thought to myself, exists in shadow. This is how we see. I wanted so much, in that very moment, to see beyond shadow. I turned and faced the Citadel, and called out in my mind for *Her* to let this happen...to lift some shadows for me.

Chapter Nine - The Philosopher

On this side of the C-T is situated an open square where public debate and discussion is held. Many come to listen to the words of such men. I have seen and heard several philosophers in my young years. They meet every time the two suns cross our planet thirty-three times. It is an opportunity for the women to come too. They listen and often I have seen them cautiously smile at such words. I am sure the women have a knowing all their own. And this knowing they keep hidden within; shared between them by coded glances and instinctual bonds. Real philosophy is in the heart, my mother once said. I am beginning to learn what this means as my mind cannot store any more words. With a mind jammed with symbols and etched ideas I have come to a standstill. Perhaps now it is only the heart that can lead me beyond this impasse. I am beginning to wonder if the time of the mind is at an end...dusty and dry like our streets outside. Fitting perhaps that I should arrive

at the quarter of this avenue where minds are formed. Here

is housed the Guild of Scholars and the Guild of

Philosophers - minds against minds. Many words thrown

about like rattling sharp steel thrusts. I have heard some

minds in debate that behave as if they are in battle. Their

words are their tools to attack and defend. Not only to do

harm, but to create a veil of untruths and emotions of

distrust. Such words are used for winning; not for

resolving. Yet I am still intrigued by these discussions.

It seems as if my young life has become that of a collector.

I have a need, it now seems to me, to collect as many

pieces of information, knowledge, and truths as I can.

Perhaps somewhere amongst this patchwork there is a

thread of real knowledge. It must be here, scattered

amongst the seeds and segments of our cluttered

civilization. Somewhere in C-T there must lay the artefacts that can help me to know more. I have a feeling such things exist throughout the known cosmos to assist us: on each habitable planet…for each civilization, human or other. It is just that they don't show themselves so openly. So I look, ask, enquire, and seek. I guess many people are used to my ways by now. They permit me access to their trade dwellings much more freely now. It often surprises me how they open up and talk to me. They talk where once there was no space, no room for their words with me. My youth can protect me. Soon I will be expected elsewhere; caught up in other duties. Then I will no longer be so welcome in the trade dwellings of others. It will be expected of me that I know my place, and remain there. The confines of C-T are more than its shadows…there are shadows within minds too.

I soon came upon the dwelling of the Philosopher. I had

already been here several times. There was something

about this man I liked. He spoke funny, almost in riddles.

Or his thoughts weaved through corridors in his mind as if

it were a personal labyrinth. For a high ranking man of

knowledge he was surprisingly kind and without too much

sense of himself. I wish there were more words to describe

such things. I feel inadequate with the shortage of words

available to me. Sometimes within people there is a strong

sense of self, yet not the real, or what I would say the

genuine self. It is like a false self - one constructed from the

outside in. It is full with one's acquired personality. And

people parade and defend this exterior self that they have. I

wish there was a word, or a better combination of words,

to describe this. I think it is also a part of people's minds. It

is a part of them that strives to please the personality. And

so they feed it; and it grows and becomes more dominant.

And yet many people do not see this big, greedy part of

their minds - or they do not wish to see it. But this

Philosopher has a milder part of his exterior personality.

Maybe he can even admit to himself when he is wrong.

I entered the dwelling quietly so not to disturb the

fluttering patterns within the philosopher's mind. People

seldom enter the dwelling of a philosopher as they have

nothing to trade. Philosophers are not overly social or

public people. They appear in public for the discussions

and debates, as is their duty. Other times they supply ideas

to the Lawgivers. Yet they remain largely private. I suppose

their trade is a more internal one. They discuss more within

themselves, and amongst themselves within their guild.

In the corner of the shadowed main room stood a large

chair. Within this chair the old Philosopher sat with eyes

closed. His body appeared to be rocking gently, as if upon the rhythmic waves of his thoughts. Or perhaps it was his chair that was rocking. It was hard to see clearly with such lack of light. I remembered from before how his old face was marked with many age-lines, and he had long white facial hair on his chin. It is known that in the Guild of Philosophers the processing time is much longer than with other guilds. A philosopher is often old by the time his public C-T duties begin. So the people of C-T are used to seeing such old men begin their obligation. In fact, we don't see any young philosophers. They are kept within the guild. I'm not sure if philosophers ever marry or have families. I do not know of such, not in my quarter of C-T. Yet in my quarter there is no such functionary; and I do not dare to ask on this matter. The Philosopher has opened his eyes, and is now peering at me from across the room. I stand still where I am.

'Ah, yes...you are back. Your mind continues to compel you. I find that most intriguing considering all and everything about you. And yet you return to listen again to me. You have an urge within you greater than most of your elders.' The Philosopher chuckled in his charming way, and I smiled back at him. Perhaps he was right. Or rather, being somewhere between right and wrong - or perhaps neither - was where the Philosopher had his territory of the mind. For me, being in the younger stage of my life, I really did not know how much effort should be extended in this being *right* or *wrong*. I'm not even sure if such exactitudes, such certainties, existed. How could they exist in human civilization - a biological artifice so impermanent?

'Come, sit here with me.' The Philosopher beckoned me to approach. I could not see him clearly as the room was darker than most dwellings. There were shadows created within to match against the natural shadows from the great wall. An overlapping of shade: to protect? To conceal? 'My mind operates more effectively within deep shadows,' said the Philosopher softly. 'When my public presence is required, I step out into the least shadow. Here, in my dwelling, where inner work is forged, I retreat into deeper shadow. Yet fear not, there are no parasites of the mind here...no viruses to infect your thoughts.' The Philosopher let out a low chuckle as I sat down on a padded chair near to him. I could not be sure that the old man could see me; yet this did not seem important to either of us. We were in presence together. People of our different classes rarely held such presence together; especially not in such close proximity as we were. As I sat there, silence engulfed us. I didn't mind this. I liked the silence. I welcomed it as a comfort. I'd been so used to silence all my life that it had become a deep friend to me. In my own silence I noticed how much other people spoke. It wasn't just that they spoke, as they needed to in everyday life. It was as if they spoke just to be speaking; like it filled some kind of gap for them. Maybe people are more afraid or nervous of spaces and silences than they realize. I liked the company of this Philosopher as he spoke only when he had something to say. He was careful with his words; even if his words were like riddles sometimes. Now I could hear him mumbling in the shadows. I could feel his chair rocking from the slight vibrations under my feet, as my sense of hearing and touch are more developed in me. Time elapsed. I do not know how long we sat in the silence of the shadows before the Philosopher spoke again.

'You are a patient one. This bodes you well, and marks you out. Ah, I was rambling through the archives of my old mind. Trying to locate the exact place where we closed our previous talk. It would be unfitting for a philosopher of my guild to start talking from just anywhere. We take honour in speaking from known locations. Now, I have found where we were last positioned. Ah yes - the meaning and purpose of our Citadel. No doubt, still a much beloved topic of yours!' The Philosopher coughed to clear his throat. I became a little more apprehensive as I sat in my padded chair. I sensed there was more the Philosopher could tell me; and wished to tell me. I could hear the slight, the very slight, tapping of the Philosopher's fingers as he drummed them together. My hearing, as I have hinted, is quite acute. 'In present days we no longer penetrate into the mysteries of our giant friend the Citadel. Yet there were other epochs when we did. There was a time when we could literally enter into her enclosed depths.' My heart almost stopped beating. Was he saying that we once were able to enter inside the Citadel? 'Much of my mind still lives in that epoch. I too am a relic from the past that permeates the present.' The Philosopher chuckled softly. 'There is much knowledge still held within the archives of the Guild of Philosophers that no longer finds a place in our world today. I fear the younger philosophers who enter our guild will not seek or penetrate into such vestiges of knowledge. These are remnants that belong to a bygone era. Yet during my apprenticeship, my Philosopher teacher passed them on to me. He too had a curiosity such as you display.'

Another silence entered our conversation like a passing guest.

'Once we had our techniques for entering into the Citadel.' The old man rocked and nodded his head in rhythm to his movement. 'Yes, we had the technologies for entering into the Citadel and into the light. It was not such an easy thing. It needed preparation and time. Yet we knew it once. Yes, we had the ways. It was a skill we learnt. It took training, just like most important things do. Yet with this special training those selected few gained a technique for shifting themselves out of C-T and into the Citadel. This was well-known at the time. Ahh, but people gradually lost this knowledge, as is always the way. It is whispered amongst the old Philosophers that there are still an unknown few who know such ways. The old Philosophers speculate on those they term the 'invisibles,' who still exist and live amongst us undetected. It is said such people know how to enter the Citadel without the body. They whisper that such technologies still remain in human knowledge - yet are hidden.' The Philosopher paused and turned his face to look directly at me. I could not be sure how much he could truly see within this shadowed room. If he could see, he would have detected my eager expression and my thirst for more. This was the first time I had ever heard of such things. It was too incredible not to want to know more. Almost too incredible to be believable.

'Yet although it is said there are — or were - a few humans who can gain access into the Citadel, the rest of us are unable to create a door, or dismantle the walls of the Citadel for others to enter. I think the real problem lies in a different door - the portal of the human mind. If we are no longer looking, or interested, in finding a real entry into the unknown we shall never know how to seek for it. The answers we receive are relative to the questions we ask. Perhaps the Citadel reflects the state of our own human civilization and our thinking as a collective whole, not just the individual. I'm afraid we Philosophers are beginning to think that our human civilization has come to a point where it no longer knows whether it is awake or dreaming. Perhaps this is all a dream - a collective hypnosis - and the Citadel is trying to wake us up. I wonder if we are inwardly lacking something important, something truly vital. And now instead of being within the Citadel we are living amongst its shadows. I fear that even the Philosophers too are becoming corrupted. Some minds have been roaming within the shadows so long that they don't know how to look in the light.' The Philosopher coughed again as if to clear his throat. Yet I detected another faint sense in this sound. That it was to protect something else. A sense of sadness perhaps?

'There was a story often told amongst the Philosophers of old. We called it "The Prince of Pleiades." It tells of a royal family that lived in a far away place known only to us as the Land of Pleiades. In this land no one lacked for anything. Everyone was content in a place which no human words are adequate to describe. Now this royal family had a son, a prince by the name of Baal. One day Baal's parents came to him and said: "Dear son, it is the custom of this land that the royal son must leave to fulfil a quest. This trial is for you to gain maturity, wisdom, and experience; so that you may return here with qualities you can use for the benefit of Pleiades. This is required in order for you to be fit to be king one day. There is no other way than this for you to acquire the skills needed. It has always been this way. Thus it has been and so it will always be." Prince Baal prepared himself for the journey, for it was to be a journey of exile. His parents provided him with special nourishment that although was of small quantity it was limitless in its sustenance. They also provided him with other special resources, for his protection, of which we do not know of, and so cannot tell. His trial required that the prince journey to a mysterious place known as Siyah Taş. He had to travel in disguise: in clothes that suited his new condition, and not that of a prince. He was also provided with guides to assist him on his journey. The prince's task was to locate and bring back a wondrous jewel that was locked away in a mighty Citadel. Prince Baal set out upon his journey and after a time his guides left him, according to their instructions. The prince was now all alone in a foreign land.

Yet soon the prince came across another traveller who was
on a similar mission. They travelled together for a time
which allowed them to keep alive the memory of their
noble origins. However, there was something about the
food and the air of Siyah Taş that gradually made them
forget about their mission as if some kind of sleep had
come upon them. For a long time after that Prince Baal
lived in Siyah Taş earning a normal living, as if he was a
regular inhabitant of that far place. He had lost all
awareness over both his true origins and his special task. By
means of which we are unaware, the prince's parents back
in the Land of Pleiades came to learn of their son's
dilemma. They devised a means whereby they would be
able to release him from his forgetful sleep so he could
continue with his mission. They were able to send a
message to the land of Siyah Taş that would activate the
prince. The message had special sounds that said "Awake,
Awake!" into the mind of the prince. This message

succeeded in awakening the prince, who immediately remembered his true self and his task. Prince Baal located the gigantic Citadel and by means of a special technique taught to him back home he entered beyond its walls and retrieved the precious jewel. Guided by the sound of the message the prince retraced his steps away from Siyah Taş and back to his homeland. He reached his home and once again dressed himself in his true princely robes. Through his experiences he was able to realize what a true and magnificent splendour was the Land of Pleiades. He now had the skills to be an exalted king in his own right. This is known as the tale of "The Prince of Pleiades.'"

The Philosopher sighed and, in the dim light, I could make out a gentle shaking of his head. The Philosopher's words had become strained towards the end; as if he too was finding it hard to remember the tale. My suspicion was confirmed when the Philosopher said, 'even that story is rarely told amongst us now. It is no longer shared.' A sad tinge seemed to permeate the air between us. We were both lost in thought and in places seldom visited. The Philosopher was straining to hold onto some hidden spark. He was breathing more heavily now; his head slightly bowed.

'It's kernel lies quietly within, awaiting another generation perhaps. Maybe one day the right generation will come along that will awaken to the call of the Citadel. Perhaps it is a story that awaits to guide us out of the shadows, out from the slumber of our minds, and back to our noble origins. I rarely tell that story now. Very few people know how to listen these days. Speaking, it seems, is all the rage. Endless speaking, endless tongues…all on top of each other. No one hears when everyone is speaking at once. I hear speaking that comes from people in bits, as if not properly connected. It is like listening to spitting. Words cut short, as if our communication is being spliced up into tiny packages. I desire the long conversations; the ones that stretch beyond the shifting of shadows - beyond the passing of the two suns. Such conversations can take us into truths. Then we take these truths into our meditations and we search for the silence that exists in the spaces between letters. In that silence also is the heart of humankind. How I long for the return of true communication within the inner silence. But now there is too much mind...too much mind.'

I felt emotion for this old Philosopher. He had spoken truly to me. I stood up and quietly walked over to where he was sitting. I bent down slightly so that our faces were at the same level. As our eyes became adjusted to the new distance between us I noticed his strong gaze. We acknowledged each other in a speechless way. It was as if human civilization had shrunk into a single limitless moment. There was everything and there was nothing. Everything existed, yet in a way unknown to us. And the Citadel awaited our awakening.

The lateness of the day fell upon me.

I departed from the Philosopher. His words and presence had entered into me like no other time previously. I made my way along the intersecting avenue back to my quarter on the other side of C-T. I passed along the Citadel walls. All the time her grand presence towered over me like a mineral heart - a precious jewel.

Chapter Ten - The Cult of Light

I arrived at my dwelling by the end of the two suns passing. It was the time all the families came back together, and trade in C-T ceased until the next rising of the two suns. It was a time when people took nourishment together. Families sometimes shared their nourishment with invited families, or single friends. Those friends especially who had lost their partner or family were encouraged to take nourishment with others. The light of our dwellings were provided by artificial lights, in special cages, that are kept under direct sunlight during the passing of the two suns. They are made to store this light, which they then give out during the period of darkness when the two suns are away from us. Our dwellings are warm. There is enough heat even in shadows. The time of nourishment is a quiet time. There is little speaking.

My father Johan is a quiet person even during busy periods. I consider Johan to be a person who is comfortable with what he quietly knows. And I suspect he knows a lot of things. Not in any specialized way, like the Scholar or the Philosopher. But in a more general way, like he knows bits from everything. I'm sure this is because of working in Archives. He stores a lot of information. Some of this must stay with him. Not the regular statistical C-T type of information, but the other stuff - the type of things not open to the public. I know sometimes he and my mother speak together quietly in whispers. I used to think it was because they did not wish to disturb me and my older brother. Now that my older brother has left the house for his apprenticeship with the Guild of Lawgivers I realize the whispers are not for us. I have a feeling that my mother is also a person who knows, although not in the same way as my father perhaps. Yet they must share information. My mother would not get access to much information once the early classes had finished. After the learning classes finish, the boys prepare for apprenticeship selection. The girls are taught further by their mothers in their dwellings. They are prepared for keeping a family. I don't think much about this. I still sense there is much the mothers, the women of C-T, don't tell us. They must know things that the men don't sense. That is the way it is. I sense this because I have a special communication with my mother. She speaks to me about the things that reach us in our dreams at night. I communicate to her also those events that my mind experiences in the night when I am sleeping. I know I must communicate to her my recent dream of the dying of the two suns.

After evening nourishment my father retreated into his work room for private study. He smiled gently at my

mother and me. I have heard it said that I resemble my
father in the face. I cannot know this. How can I see my
own face?

Under the glow of our dwelling light I communicated to
my mother the dream that affected me so much. She
watched and followed me intently, without interruption.
She nodded her head when I had finished. I saw a glassy
look in her eyes. I sense there is some other remembrance
in her mind that is drawn out by my dream. Perhaps she is
making connections with some other event. I can feel
something. When I had finished the special communication
between us, my mother sat quietly for a long time. We both
endured the silence. There appeared a strange expression
on my mother's face. Something like sadness mixed in with
a recognition, a knowing.

'What you have communicated to me touches me deep within. It also saddens me. And yet it is not a vision unexpected to me - nor to your father. We have tried to keep you protected from our thinking. I see now there is something inside of you - in your deeper self - that connects to us stronger than words and learning. This is something C-T life cannot take out of you. It is within your self just as it has been within us. It is a sense of things. A sense when things are not right, not in balance. It is also a need to know more. I sense you have this calling within you.' My mother approached a little closer to me and lowered her voice.

'I have recognized for some time now that you are interested in the Citadel. It interests us too, your father and I. We know there is something more important that has to do with the Citadel. And it is connected with us...with us as a human civilization. We know so little, and we are told even less. Information has been kept from us. It has also been lost from us. So much we once knew and now we know not. Yet there are some of us who wish to keep the Tradition alive.' I was not sure exactly what my mother meant. A look of incomprehension must have rippled discreetly across my face.

'There have been those who have always known about the Citadel. There is a knowledge that lives still, even now. It is no coincidence that in your dream you spoke of the Cult of Light.' I nodded my head in acknowledgment. I had heard snippets about this group from time to time. The last time I had heard someone speak of the Cult of Light was the Smithy when he had shown me the strange instruments he was asked to make for them. Yet this had been after my dream. 'The Cult of Light exists to keep in continuation the true knowledge about the Citadel...well, whatever knowledge that remains. We had a teacher once. We refer to him solely as Prophet. Here was a person who came to us from the stars - as light dressed in rags. Rags of multi-colours. He told us the truth. He told us that we are all beings of light dressed within the rags of our flesh. Prophet told us too that there are beings of light who exist in the Citadel. It is from them that the Citadel has an eternal inner light. It is this light that pours at night from the high windows. Yet no one can enter inside the Citadel. There are no doors and no way in. It is said that the beings of light in the Citadel are waiting for a time when humanity is ready to be reunited with their own light. This will be a time when we have dispelled our shadows of greed, desire, and hatred. In C-T people forget. They have forgotten they are beings of light. And we are now forbidden to speak or even think of such things. Prophet was declared a madman - a man made crazy by the heat of the two suns. He was banished and removed from the avenues of C-T. It is said he was taken into exile to live amongst the sun mutants. This was his punishment for speaking of what is truly within us. Now we speak only of outside things. There is no language, no words, for that which is within.'

My mother fell back into silence. Her words vibrated within me. It was a sudden explosion of colour filaments. I felt sparkles run through my body. It was my body that was reacting to these words; as if sending me a message that these words had found their counterpart in some place within me. Then my mind lit up. My mother had been using the word 'we' all this time. My eyes widened. The Cult of Light. My mother...my father?

'Yes, my child, your father and I belong to the Cult of Light. Your father's findings in the Archives first led us upon this path. Your father found the remnants of this tradition. It has always existed amongst us. We are sure there are those whom we cannot see that walk among us.

Perhaps there are others who walk among other planets - in

other civilizations out there amidst the stars. All we know is

that we have a Citadel here with us, here upon this planet.

We are its children. It is said the Citadel arose when people

forgot they were part of a grander, sacred order. Prophet

said that our arrogance denied us access, and closed us off

from the source within. Within the Archives it is written

that Prophet told the people that if the lights inside the

Citadel stopped shining, we would all die. It would be as if

the suns had gone out. The Citadel light is like the light

inside us that sustains both us and C-T. Without this light

the human being grows without nourishment. Our

forgetfulness serves to strengthen the walls of the Citadel,

and deny us access. Really, is there anyone who can

remember a time before the Citadel was built? Or

remember a time during its construction? Or knows of

anyone from past history who spoke of these things?

Perhaps we have no history. Or maybe these things never happened. Possibly there has never been a time when there was no Citadel. So how did it come to be here...who are the original builders? Of this the Archives say nothing. They are silent. Or their record has been permanently erased. We have been left with almost nothing.'

My mother's face showed concern, mixed with frustration and that energy of the heart-mind we call emotion. I sensed that she had waited so long to tell me this. Why the reticence, I wondered. Was the subject so difficult, so secretive? I had heard of the Cult of Light, yet had never known nor met anyone who confessed belonging to it. I recalled how in my dream they spoke of the dying of the two suns. Yet I had assumed this was just imagination. Now here, in my very family - my own parents who brought me into life and raised me - was a source, a direct link to the Cult of Light. The profundity and shock of this revelation suddenly hit me. I found myself unable to communicate. I could only stare at my mother with wide eyes of countless questions. I noticed a slight twitch in my mother's body. It was then that I sensed an inner desire in her to reach out to me and to hold me. Yet she pulled back and restrained her desire. Finally, she reached out her hand and held mine, in an act of rare intimacy. I was so glad of the connection; of hearing her speak her truth. I grasped her hand back as a gesture to urge her to continue.

'There must be change, renewal. Without this, the Cult of Light does not see a future. Yet change does not occur through the majority, or through our systems of power. It comes through the unexpected, the anomalies - the disruption to existing ways. Change is created through a few individuals who walk a different path - like Prophet did. Such individuals are like mutants. Not mutants of the past or present, but mutants of the future. There must be a difference in things - difference matters! And difference is also a danger. Those in power do not like difference. They do not wish for change. That is why we nurture the difference within us. It grows within our selves, as if also a part of our biology. If we were to manifest difference in our lives outside, in our trades, we would be banished. Yet more and more of us are feeling this difference now - this *urge*. It is time for something new, something disruptive, to arrive into C-T.'

I listened intently to all that my mother was saying. I did not fully understand the meaning behind her words, yet I sensed I knew what she was trying to communicate to me. I too had felt the restrictions in life around me. Some of them are visible, and they are provided by our Lawgivers. Yet there is so much that is not visible; these are the

restrictions that flow below the surface. They lie beneath
the unspoken assumptions - the fears, the unchanging
rituals and ways of thinking. They lie embedded in the
Guilds and the ways of things that have been with us so
long. And for me especially, they lie within the
unquestioning, the unknowing, and the uncaring silence
that surrounds our Citadel.

'Your dream. It is so important!' My mother looked at me
with insisting eyes. It felt as if she was reaching for
something inside of me...to pull at something, or to open
something. 'I, or rather your father and I, we both
recognized your interest in the Citadel. This same
recognition has not manifested in your older brother. Yet
we saw how it came through into you. We have been
watching it. We have seen how you gaze out at the Citadel
and its walls. You look up at the high windows where the
eternal light shines from. You observe how the walls form

the mighty shadows that shade and protect C-T. Don't you want to go inside the Citadel?' I nodded my head slowly. Everything my mother said had been right. I had not noticed their attention on me. Did my parents also wish to enter into the Citadel? I remembered the words spoken earlier by the Philosopher. There had once been technologies, techniques for entering the Citadel. What had he said...people once knew how to leave their bodies? Did my parents know of this?

'There are no doors. There has never been any visible way into the Citadel. Does this not tell you something? A great building, with lighted windows, and yet no obvious way in. How can it be a normal building? Its purpose must be something other, and so must be the way to gain entry. The Cult of Light recognizes this, has always recognized this. And yet people here do not question - they do not *see*. We wonder if there is amnesia amongst us...' My mother's

voice trailed off into a distant thought. Her gaze moved
over to the wall of our dwelling where beyond lay the
Citadel outside. We were dwelling as if under its rocky
wings. 'We of the Cult of Light came together as a way to
remember. To help those who wanted to remember, to
learn again what they knew they had forgotten before it's
too late. Before the Citadel lights go out forever. Until then
it waits…and we wait. We wait until we can regain the
technologies of entry. Such a technology lies with us - lies
within us.'

My mother motioned for me to remain where I was while
she prepared some warm zeedar, our night infusion.
Suddenly, in this small moment, I felt the scale of space
and time. How our moment in it is so staggeringly small;
and yet so immensely precious. I felt entangled within a
complex paradox that was of unknowing simplicity. How

insufficient are words! Words belong to the Guild of Tokeners, to be traded and circulated as objects. They are insufficient for the understanding of truths.

My mother and I sipped our warm, soothing zeedar. Its taste helps to remind us of home - our planetary home. It seems to connect us together, our bodies and the body of the planet. I always sleep well after this drink. I also dream well. Maybe too it is the body of the planet that influences my dreams. I sense we are all connected in ways not yet understood by us.

Right at that moment I felt a strong emotion...no, not emotion; it was more like energy. I felt it rise up within me, rising through my body. I almost felt as if I had reached out and touched the stars. I sensed a heat in my face. For the second time that evening my mother reached out and touched my hand. I appreciated the touch. I realized how missing it was from our lives. I suddenly had a remembrance of my own behaviour during the day. I too had felt the need to reach out to those who had communicated with me. It was as if an urge to make a real connection. And to hide the gesture within a fleeting touch, if possible.

'There is a special person amongst us who knows more. We of the Cult of Light reach out for his guidance. This is a great secret within our tradition. He is said to be descended from the one who was Prophet, the one who was thought a madman, a crazy fool. After he was banished from C-T he must have raised a family amongst the sun mutants. Prophet's descendent lives among us now, at this very time. He has the symbol which was handed down by Prophet and kept throughout his lineage. In each epoch, each generation, there has always been a descendent of Prophet living and working amongst us here in C-T. This person makes themselves known in each generation to those who are able to understand.' My mother's voice was now in a whisper. Perhaps she feared the walls of our dwelling were as perforated ears. Or there was something in the air that could catch her speech and run away with it like an invisible thief. 'Throughout our history the Cult of Light has been contacted by this individual and taught by them. We must be careful though. Last time was banishment for Prophet. I fear this time it would be worse.'

Yes. This was what I needed to know. My body trembled.

'You did not know this, yet we encouraged you to visit and speak with this individual; the teacher of our age. To our surprise, and delight, you have been returning many times. He tells us that you have much capacity within you. He has

told you things few people ever hear. Perhaps you did not
know this, or recognize it, since you are still young. Your
mind is still fresh enough not to form opinion. Yet we have
all noticed this, especially your father and I. You have been
growing upon these words. Your mind and body have been
fed different nourishment – the nourishment of meaning.
There is a different growth in you…a true difference. And
yet it is organic and natural.' My mother now paused and
smiled at me in a wondrous way. A way of love.

'Can you sense who this individual is? Do you feel now
who has been your true teacher?'

Instantly I knew. Yes, I could sense it. I could *feel* it. Of
course. It could be no other.

Chapter Eleven - The Beekeeper

I watched him hobble around his studio. The old man.

Things from before now seemed to fit into place. I

remembered him saying once that 'the secret protects

itself'... and it had been right before my eyes. I had always

trusted my senses. I thought my senses were more

developed in me because of the way I communicate. And

yet this I had not sensed. My teacher eyed me silently from

a corner of the room as he shuffled through a collection of

his drawings. I was sure he was smiling, or even laughing,

inside of himself.

'Ah, yes, there it is!' The old man pulled out a drawing from

his cluttered collection. He held it up for me to see. It was a

beautifully crafted line drawing of a most unusual and

exquisite bird. It was a bird I did not recognize. The old

man noticed my inquisitive and confused look. 'It is the phasal bird. You were here when the man came in to commission it.' Yes, I remembered now. It was a large man who had come to ask for a drawing of the rare phasal bird. I'm not even sure if such a bird exists. The Calligrapher had known at once what a phasal bird looked like. He had asked the man to come back when thirty dawns of our two suns had passed. This had stuck in my mind. Both the large man and I thought it an unusually long time. And yet here the drawing was, and so little time had passed. The Calligrapher chuckled to himself. 'That man who came, he really didn't need a phasal bird drawing. What he needed was time. So I gave him time - thirty dawns of our two suns of it! He'll get his bird as well, but he won't be needing it.' The Calligrapher placed the drawing back into the pack and went back to his desk. His hunched figure bent over the table and continued to sort through his drawing instruments. He picked out one and dipped it into a bowl of drawing liquid, then slowly held it up to his face.

'Drawing, creating, is a release. It's a release from the mind that traps us. In this age we are trapped in a thinking that moves like a straight line.' The Calligrapher drew a straight line across his canvas. 'It is a thinking that helps us to do things that are rational. It all comes from this thing we have up here.' The old man tapped his head with the end of his drawing instrument. 'Yet after a time this type of straight line thinking dries up. It dries up because it only knows one direction. And when that direction has done all that it can, it needs a different path. Yet straight line thinking doesn't know how to change. Change can bring possibilities we find hard to imagine. And it can bring danger for those who don't wish to imagine change. Yet the only real thing we have is movement - everything flows! This is life. And now we need a thinking that reflects this fluid understanding.' The Calligrapher took his instrument and drew some circular abstract lines on the canvas that wove in-between themselves. Within a few vivid moments he had drawn what looked to be a ball as it did not look flat. It seemed to jump out of the canvas, as if it was real. As if it had sides to it. Or it wasn't a ball. It was perhaps a planet, with crossing lines that intersected. I could not say truly. Yet the image mesmerized me.

'We have to change how we see things before we can change things as they are. We cannot create that which lies outside of our capacity to understand. C-T draws upon the familiar, the stable. We have come to the end of the stable in our epoch. We must see things differently now.' I walked over to the collection of drawings and began carefully to look through them. Many of the drawings were of familiar images - animals, buildings, objects - and yet they were represented in a different way. There was something remarkably unfamiliar about them. I sensed now what the Calligrapher had been saying. It was all about how we *looked* at the world. It was this *looking* that defined our thinking. It shaped our attitudes, beliefs, and opinions.

'People come here to ask me for one thing. I provide them with their wishes, and yet I also provide another thing. Their attention is relieved by what they believe is the image they requested. Yet within the familiarity that they crave is also something else that enters them from below their level of attention. My drawings seep into their minds through another door. People are asleep, and do not know that they are. They are like the great Citadel you are so fond of. On the exterior they are a closed building. There are no doors or obvious entry points. There is a light that burns within yet cannot be reached. The human - like the Citadel - was designed to be awakened. And yet the Citadel's only use as we know it is for the shadows we live within. Humans too are these shadows.' The bent figure of the Calligrapher

slowly stepped out of the room. When he did not return

after some moments I left to look for him. His dwelling

had few rooms. It was a modest building. I always thought

the Calligrapher lived alone. A door in the opposite wall of

his food preparation room was ajar. I had not noticed this

door before. I walked slowly toward it and peered around

the door. On the other side was a small open courtyard. I

stepped through. In the middle of this courtyard there

stood a compact tree with small leaves. The fruit of the tree

was hanging like balls that opened out into a strange

flower-like spout. The Calligrapher was seated against a

wall of the courtyard. I was not expecting to see such a

place, hidden away at the heart of the dwelling. There was a

second chair placed beside the old man, as if waiting for me

- or for someone? Without communication I walked over

and sat beside the Calligrapher.

In silence we sat, opposite the tree. Finally the Calligrapher

spoke, as if waiting for my eyes to finish their observation

of this fruit tree. 'It is called a Granada tree. Its fruit has

many pockets of seeds inside. The fruit can be eaten or

drunk. It gives us great health, yet we must first give the

fruit our time. Without the right time there cannot be the

correct health. The tree also requires something that is

beyond our grasp. It requires sunlight. Here in this

courtyard the sunlight reaches in for a short time as it

passes from zenith to setting. It passes just long enough to

provide the correct amount of sunlight, and just short

enough not to burn. It is this right amount of exposure that

is necessary. The courtyard was designed to be a place to

provide for this right amount. Right quantities are

extremely important. The right amount of light and shade

is also important. The people of C-T have become too

accustomed to the shadows. There is a deep disharmony

that needs to be rebalanced. We have become trapped by our very selves. What we created now becomes a prison for us. People have lost the knowledge of their own creation.' I gave the old man a quick look. I was not sure of his meaning. I wondered if he was speaking in riddles. The old man smiled. It was a gentle, honest smile, so distinct from his crooked physical frame. 'I speak of the Citadel - your beloved Citadel. The Citadel was built brick by brick by humans as we gradually began to forget and fall into sleep. The more we slept the taller the Citadel became. Its walls were built by our ideologies, by our beliefs and power structures – by all of our thoughts that separated us from our true origins. The Citadel has no doors because it is a reflection of us. It cannot be dismantled, or entered into, by the same thinking that brought it into being. We live in the shadow of the Citadel because it is *us*.'

Within the courtyard there was no view of the Citadel. We were shielded from it. All windows led directly into an interior room. I was so used to being able to see the Citadel directly, either from where I was or from the nearest window. Yet now I realised, for the first time in my young life, that there could be a separation from the Citadel. I also had the distinct sense that the shadow was lighter here. I turned to look at the Calligrapher. He was an odd figure. People came to him because he had a special skill. He could give them something else, something needed and yet unbeknown to them.

'You think about the light inside of the Citadel. That too is a reflection of us. And this light can be extinguished if no one exists to recognize it. That is why there must always be those amongst us who can keep the light within humanity burning. This is the signature of responsibility that has been handed down, generation after generation. It is a signature of true remembrance.' The Calligrapher raised his hand and pointed to the far wall of the courtyard. I did not understand what he wanted me to see. I focused my attention. And then I saw it - a symbol carved into the wall. Subtle, almost unnoticeable, and yet so clearly there.

'The symbol was handed down to us long, long ago. Its tradition goes back farther than any of us know. Even Prophet could not say where its origins lay. He would only say it came to us from the stars. And like a star that shines in our skies, in every epoch there is a visible guide for those who know how to look. We must each of us be guided by our own star. We are not alone. There has always been a community. Without such a community, life would cease. A true community is needed to pollinate our growth. This is what we mean by evolution. It is not the accidental or random Forming. It is a known design that works through us. And there are those that know the patterns. Just like the story I told you earlier about the prisoner and the rug. We must learn to see the designs and patterns laid out before us. Then we can know. And with this knowledge we can move forward with understanding and intention. I speak to you now about the community of the Beekeepers.'

In the silence of the courtyard I listened intently to the words of the Calligrapher.

'There is still a distant memory of a person called Prophet who is revered by those of the Cult of Light. This person was indeed my ancestor. He was entrusted with the mandate to keep alive and pass on the knowledge of humankind's origins. And also to keep safe the knowledge of how humankind may help itself, and thus be aligned with the patterns of the cosmos. Yet Prophet should not be revered in the way he is. There is a danger that the personality eclipses the message. When people crave attention rather than knowledge, they too easily attach themselves to a strange personality, or to a personality with power. There is a real danger that the Cult of Light may go this way. That is why it is important that individuals - like you and me - can meet and communicate face to face. There is work that can be done with and between groups, and there is work that requires an individual contact. The Cult of Light operates as a kind of filter mechanism. Those who are attracted to a residual trace of knowledge are first attracted to this group. It is then my function to extract

those who show a capacity for further development. I

communicate with each person according to their capacity

to understand. There is nothing general about what I do.'

The Calligrapher paused, as if to allow me time to digest his

words - his meaning.

'In our work, change is one of the most important things.

A person must be able to perceive the need for change, and

also to perceive the connections when change occurs.

There is a need to grasp a sense of the bigger picture, and

how this connects to events and situations in our everyday,

individual lives. True work can only operate with the right

people, in the right place, at the right time. There is a

precision through which the science of humankind

operates. What so few of us realize is that we owe a great

debt. Until we can feel this debt deep within us, and the

responsibility of our service, it is very difficult for further development. Our deepest need is to move forward, and to make efforts toward developing ourselves. And yet our personal development must be in harmony with a greater need. Yet you cannot know this greater need. However, there is a community that does know, and has always known. This is the Community of Beekeepers.'

My first reaction to this statement was one of unfamiliarity combined with a tingling sensation within me at learning that such a community did indeed exist. The familiar and the unfamiliar mixed in me like two rivers that meet and form a vortex of whirling energy. I had never heard the word *beekeeper* before.

'A beekeeper is one who looks after and nurtures bees. Bees are tiny winged creatures that are not known on this planet. They are similar to the little winged *baals* that we have here. These bees collect a certain substance from various flowers, and accumulate and store this substance in their community dwelling. The Beekeepers say that knowledge is like this substance that the bees collect. Like the bees they store this knowledge in a specially constructed place, and release it into the world when the time is right. Or, they release it to certain individuals who show a special capacity to work with this knowledge for the betterment of humankind. So it has been, and so it will always be. The Beekeepers say that this is the true work of humanity, and that such a work produces a sweet essence.'

The Calligrapher slapped me on my knee as he stood up and hobbled away. I was shocked by this action, so unaccustomed was I to this type of touch. Yet it served to snap me out of my slight reverie that I had slipped into whilst listening to the old man speak. It also made me remember his final words - *work produces a sweet essence.*

I found the Calligrapher in the food preparation room adjoining the courtyard. He was heating an infusion for us to drink. When mixed with leaves, and sweetened, such a drink was very refreshing for us. I watched as he worked with concentrated attention. He did not communicate again, with either looks or words, until the brew was ready and poured into receptacles for us to drink. We sat down in his reception room, with its open door giving us a view of the avenue. We were now in a more public area of his dwelling.

'In your heart you know where the Beekeepers store their knowledge - the vessel that keeps this sweet essence safe until a time is needed for its release.'

Through the doorway of the Calligrapher's dwelling the great walls of the Citadel pushed shadows upon us like a protective veil. I nodded my head.

'We must seek for that release - to make it possible. In each moment we are involved in the flow of connection. It enters into you all the time. You must take possession of it and make it your own. This force is one of the few things that can help the work to find its rightful place.'

We sat in silence until our drinking vessels were empty. Nothing more was said, or communicated. It felt time to leave. I stood up to make my way out. The Calligrapher too raised himself slowly from his seat. His bent figure disguised almost perfectly the pure shape that dwelt within him. In his quiet manner he had made himself invisible. Well, invisible to those who could not see. We walked together to the outer doorway of his dwelling.

'You must remember that effort, real effort, is never lost - only that some things may not go the way you plan or expect. Do not be disappointed in this. You will now go your own way according to your capacities. We begin by means of things we can grasp. What is known acts as a bridge towards the unknown.' The old man gently touched me upon the arm and gave the sweetest of smiles. There was a deep charm in his face.

'Who would ever suspect? A lame hunchback like me, and a mute girl such as yourself.'

I smiled as I walked away. Yes, who would ever suspect the truth in such things?

Chapter Twelve – A New Beginning

It could have been another dream. It could have been real
life. Each day I was filled with both. The world does not
know what it needs. Yet there is a way that I can know.
Once a tiny drop of sweet essence has been tasted there is
no going back. I could not speak, and yet I wished to speak
the truth. This sincerity was the first step on my way to
finding the Community of Beekeepers. It had begun...

Printed in Great Britain
by Amazon.co.uk, Ltd.,
Marston Gate.